Winne...

THE GEORG...
FICTION PRIZE

Astro-biologically capacious and hypnotically drawn,

CHURN is a luminous, dense star that collapses upon itself in order to expand into its ever-widening, swelling, coming-of-age, lacunal sphere— its complex, difficult futurehood.

Within its magnetic, compelling, centrifugal, childhood/adolescent/adult cosmos, the work presents the queerest, the quasi-Asianest, and the agriculturally farmiest of semi-Korean-shaded familial grief (maternal torture and paternal despair and inexorable divorce and intransigent abuse and damage and dysfunctionality) in the most poly-monochromatic fashion. rich in art and emotional, lacustrine, interstellar, eccentric, gay materials.

Designed to hold readers hostage, CHURN is a spell-binding book.

An indispensable antidote to hopelessness.

— VI KHI NAO, CONTEST JUDGE

and author of *Funeral,*
Swimming with Dead Stars,
and *A Brief Alphabet of Torture*

More Praise

I can't remember ever having read a book like this. Every chapter in *Churn* will move you, surprise you, keep you on your toes. Chloe Seim is a writer of gargantuan talent, and this wonderful debut is all the proof of that we could ask for.

—ROBERT LONG FOREMAN, author of
Weird Pig, Among Other Things, and
I Am Here to Make Friends

Chloe Seim's *Churn* triumphantly reimagines the American west in the Gameboy era. The daughter of an alcoholic Kansas-born father and a South Korean mother, Jordan believes, 'The country had given me every good thing in my life.' And yet, like the homesteaders in Willa Cather's *My Antonia,* Jordan and her brother Chung must fight to preserve that goodness amid the harsh realities of plains life and their own tumultuous family history. It's a searing and original portrait from a bright new voice in American literature."

—WHITNEY TERRELL, author of
The Good Lieutenant,
The King of Kings County,
and *The Huntsman*

for CHURN

A dazzling debut from an explosive and versatile writer. Seim's prose will incinerate you with its memorable characters and fearless tackling of Korean-American identity, coming of age while poor in rural Kansas, and the mythical—borderline supernatural—way some children metabolize the legacy of family and environmental traumas they inherit...and are forced to continually confront it in adulthood. Equal parts protest and fairy tale, *Churn* is unapologetic and fiercely creative. Authentic and innovative. Not a book you want to miss!

—TARA STILLIONS WHITEHEAD, author of
They More Than Burned

Written in prose by turns stark, playful, and inventive, *Churn* paints a bittersweet and emotionally gripping portrait of two siblings as they navigate violence, bigotry, inherited trauma, and moments of glittering joy. In both her writing and her illustrations, Seim deftly captures the feeling of a family in descent, and how the smallest discoveries—a talent for art, a glimpse at a better future—can become a foundation for survival. *Churn* is one of the best books about life in Kansas I've ever read. This one will stay with me.

—BECKY MANDELBAUM, author of
The Bright Side Sanctuary for Animals

CHURN

AN ILLUSTRATED NOVEL IN STORIES

Winner of

THE GEORGE GARRETT FICTION PRIZE

Selected by

VI KHI NAO

Established in 1998, The George Garrett Fiction Prize highlights one book per year for excellence in a short story collection or novel.

~ ~ ~ RECENT WINNERS ~ ~ ~

J. E. Sumerau, *Transmission*
Jenny Shank, *Mixed Company*
William Black, *In the Valley of the Kings*
Susan Lowell, *Two Desperados*
Jim Kelly, *Pitchman's Blues*
James Ulmer, *The Fire Doll*
Jeff P. Jones, *Love Give Us One Death*
Kathy Flann, *Get A Grip*
Stephen March, *The Gold Piano*
Tim Parrish, *The Jumper*
Starner Jones, *Purple Church*
David Armand, *The Pugilist's Wife*
Richard Spilman, *The Estate Sale*

CHURN

~ ~ ~ AN ILLUSTRATED NOVEL IN STORIES ~ ~ ~

CHLOE CHUN SEIM

TRP: The University Press of SHSU
Huntsville · Texas
texasreviewpress.org

Library of Congress Cataloging-in-Publication Data
Names: Seim, Chloe Chun, 1991- author and illustrator
Title: Churn : an illustrated novel-in-stories / Chloe Chun Seim.
Description: First edition. | Huntsville : TRP: The University Press of
SHSU, [2023] | "Winner of The 2022 George Garrett Fiction Prize."
Identifiers: LCCN 2023014108 (print) | LCCN 2023014109 (ebook) |
ISBN 9781680033496 (paperback) | ISBN 9781680033502 (ebook)
Subjects: LCSH: Adult children of dysfunctional families--Fiction. |
Adult children of immigrants--Kansas--Fiction. | Farm life--Kansas--
Fiction. | Kansas--Fiction. | LCGFT: Bildungsromans. | Linked stories.
Classification: LCC PS3619.E4254 C49 2023 (print) | LCC PS3619.
E4254 (ebook) | DDC 813/.6--dc23/eng/20230414
LC record available at https://lccn.loc.gov/2023014108
LC ebook record available at https://lccn.loc.gov/2023014109
FIRST EDITION
Illustrations by Chloe Chun Seim
Cover & Book Design: PJ Carlisle
Cover photo: Sonny Mauricio on Unsplash
"Six Days of Peace" photo: Jeanne Holborn Ritta
Author photo: Joshua Lee Robinson
Printed and bound in the United States of America

TRP: The University Press of SHSU
Huntsville Texas
texasreviewpress.org

for Michael, Mom, and Dad

CONTENTS

SINK — xiii

DRIFT — 47

SURFACE — 111

I.

SINK

Wilson Lake

The Sister

WILSON LAKE

CHUNG, a gray speck in the mauve Kansas twilight, flails, arms raised, five hundred feet from the farm. He's been in the mud for an hour. I watch him sinking, shrieking, rubber boots ten inches deep and unlikely to be set free without our parents' help. I should've told our parents right away when it happened (whichever one of them could function enough to stand). I should've helped him, my little brother.

Instead, I sit on our front porch and feel the prick of the passing storm. I ignore the frenzied begging of the cats swarming me and think, *What a good punishment this is for the bad thing he's done.* Last night, he brought my favorite stuffed tabby into the bath or played with it and dropped it in the toilet or let the dog (who isn't supposed to be inside) drag the plush thing around in its drooly mouth. It doesn't matter. The toy's faux fur crimped. Its voice box broke. No more *I love you*s. No more *You're-purrtastic*s—just a low, buzzy hiss where sweet joy once sang—and so I let the earth swallow him.

This land has a way of bending you to its will whether you are deserving or not.

AS the light, swollen with humidity, passes away, and the coyotes begin their summons, I go inside. I search for our father (whose sun-striped arms can lift Chung easily) and find him in the basement—legs sprawled, mouth open, saliva pooled, snore rapturous—unreachable, adorned with a brown-bottle halo. I locate our mother in the bedroom, similarly useless—glued to the television, latest criminal newscast—unresponsive. Finally, in the cold moonless black, my own boots catch in the divots of our long-forgotten field (which once bred corn and alfalfa and wheat), and more than once I trip—feed my fingers to the earth and come up brown. The coyotes laugh. Somewhere, deep in the woods to the south, a growl rolls, and for a moment I wonder if the mountain lion and all her cubs have returned. They made so many killings the year before.

I find Chung eventually, on his knees and silent now; the chill has stripped his cheeks white, and a look of anticipated demise swells in his eyes—until he sees me. His face shrivels. He begins to cry and reaches out to me like an infant to its mother. I tug his wrists.

I pull and pull. Nothing.

I tell him to shift all his weight forward. I heave. Pant. Nothing.

We struggle and slip and try to upturn this defiant earth. I make my plea to the soil. Offer one of the cats in return. Nothing.

Finally, the both of us sweaty and breathless, Chung forfeits his boots and follows the squish-squish of mine, curls his frigid fingers around my shirt tail. Flopping back to the farmhouse in his socks, his jeans too, are thick and black by the time we reach the porch. My hands and arms stained with mud. Chung strips his pants outside, and I take off my boots, leaving them on the steps for the cats, the dozens of them, to herd around and mark. A few adolescents sprint up, try but don't succeed in entering the house as we slip through the door quick. They rise on their hind legs, paws pressed to the screen, eyes peering, begging for refuge.

They lack the understanding that living inside brings: no refuge exists here.

Our parents haven't noticed our absence. They haven't stirred. But we have an early day tomorrow, so Chung and I crawl into our beds. Tomorrow is our final attempt at resuscitation. Tomorrow we all drive to Wilson Lake.

OUR father usually speeds, whistles as he sends that needle higher, but today as we head westward, he stays below the limit. Tries to be good. He glances at me in the rear-view mirror, and as always my body rebels, I smile, hide the anxiety, anger, dread that cooks in me like a witch's brew. He smiles back.

Our mother, meditative or over-prescribed, slumps against the passenger window. Chung bites his tongue, slays Octorok-after-Octorok in his quest for the all-powerful Triforce. I stare out into the dissolving plains. Vegetation browns. Hundred-year-old houses resist the wind, which pushes our truck side to side. That, or our father has snuck in a few beers again after all.

His proposition that we all take a few days off (from school and work) to go to the lake, came earlier this week at a desperate moment; though it was last harvest, when our father was drunk every day and driving the tractor, that "the final incident" (as our mother liked to threaten) had actually occurred. He had backed over Chung, breaking his arm into a million bits. And now *again,* a few nights ago, after months of silence, our mother dragged it up; our father had been drunk for days again, so they argued again, and the shouting was so great—as her physical might met with his, our parents (two fourth-degree Tae Kwon Do black belts) hands-to-throats in their waltz across the kitchen tile—that it brought the cops. Or rather this dance—which led little Chung (trying to break them up) to accidentally be shoved, to tumble down the long staircase—and my subsequent screams into the wet spring air (that I didn't remember, that I didn't mean to release) that alarmed the neighbors, who brought the cops.

Either way, Chung was fine, of course. Bruised and stabbed by the centimeter-long carpet nails outlining the edges of each stair, points exposed through shoddy shag rug, but he was fine. Both our parents spent the night in county jail, and our father's parents came dreary- and red-eyed to put us to sleep. And *once again,* in the morning, on their return, the apologies came also. To my mother. To each other. To us. It was during this desperate moment (the *"absolutely* final incident") when our father proposed a trip to the lake, which, like all his other half-assed, bloodshot pleas, didn't impress us, but he insisted.

WHEN we arrive, we find few other campers. None of our parents' regular camp friends are here. Late March, post-Spring Break, and following a thorough downpour, we are sure to be alone. I curse the rain and pray that others might come, might give me an out.

Our father decides to kick off things with a boat ride, so he backs the RV and its rickety boat-towing trailer to one of the small docks near our campsite. He releases the boat, its tired mass bobbing into the lake, casting small waves outward. The boat is one of many pricy, useless things our parents bought when the money was good two or three years ago.

On the water, our mother sits in the stern, the very back, silent. Once, one or two or three years ago, she might've driven the boat or danced to the radio or gone tubing with Chung or me. Once, when we weren't so unwilling to show our happiness together. Now, it has become a clotted thing; anger-restricted but potent when released. And because I can feel a loosening, I focus on the wind and the waves and the roar of the engine. An unusual heat has swarmed in but the lake's as cold as ever. Chung and I lean over the sides, let the murk spray into our mouths as our father steers and Woohoos! We swim and dive, coming up brown, teeth chattering. After an hour, it starts to feel like we're on the mend. That sneaking deception. Like all those nail-pricks and bone-splits are decades behind us.

Back at the RV for lunch, our father fires up the Coleman propane stove outside on the camp table and heats up baked beans from the can and loads cut-up hot dogs into the pot. We drink Mountain Dew and savor its silt layering our teeth. We enrich ourselves on salt and sugar. Our mother tans, or sleeps, by the beach.

As if attuned, the moment our cheeriness wavers, our father intervenes.

"How about fishing?" One of his-and-my earliest traditions—leaving every poor bluegill and carp of our favorite lakes, rivers, shallow ponds and creeks scarred and skittish.

Chung wails at the mention. He believes, has always said (though not always in such adult words) that fishing is barbaric. That it's cruelty.

And though I always fish with our father, I always think (can't help it) about what terror we are creating. Poor things. Being reeled in, wriggling for dear life, and watching your blood coil in streams behind you. How it's all a rouse. You'll be released, and each day you'll bite again and again, your mouth scarred to shit. Your stomach empty. How at some point you must pray for death. *Please, dear Fish God, let this be the time I get eaten by the land demons.*

"Chung," our father says, "why don't you go swimming again and let your mother rest? Jordan, you and me can catch us some dinner."

I think of telling him that letting a nine-year-old swim unattended is a terrible idea, but I don't. I follow our father to a cliff's edge. His fishing spot of choice, because at this height there's little chance of scaring the fish off. I also like to think that he prefers it for its precarity, sitting fifty feet above the water, jagged rocks waiting below. He's always had a daredevil's soul.

I try my best at fishing. My best is shit.

Phase two in our father's unspoken plan, it seems, is getting each of us alone. He's irritable now. I can see it. His hands shake because he hasn't had a drink since last night. He gives me the obligatory "how's school?" and "any cute boys?" and I shrug them away. He tries to win me because this is his way of dealing with screw-ups. I won't give him that.

In just two hours he manages to catch twelve fish: four bluegills, six catfish, two pikes. Over two long hours, I catch one, a bluegill runt who doesn't even flap for freedom. Its eye stays on me. *Why fight it?* it asks me.

We return empty-handed, because Chung refuses to eat freshly caught fish and because today even I find them disgusting, the whole lake reeking of death, that manmade sort of misery, and because our father, for all his farming, gets squeamish when he has to clean them.

When we return, Chung is sitting in a camping chair and playing his Gameboy. Our mother sleeps in the RV. Our father fries onion rings, asking Chung and I to do the prep. Our fingers cake with egg and flour and we swipe at each other, trying to smear the mixture over each other's faces until we both have wet mustaches. Our father fries the rings in a cast iron nested into the live firepit and grills burgers on the stove. Chung opens a bag of Lays wavy chips. When dinner's ready, I wake my mother, who tries to flatten her hair as she stands. She doesn't see it yet. I can't tell her. Her coarse black hair has knotted like a fist, no way to untangle. She'll have to cut it out.

She sinks into one of our nylon camping chairs and I take another. Chung and our father join us, our chairs circled around the fire, our hands trying to keep our flimsy paper plates from caving.

"Perfect camping weather." Our father slaps his knees. "Lake's beautiful this time of year. I don't know why no one else is out here," he says to all of us and none of us.

I don't tell him it's because of the rain and the humidity and because it's the middle of the week.

"Chung, you really need to go fishing with us next time."

"He doesn't like fishing," I say.

"It teaches you patience. It's a good learning experience."

"He doesn't want to," I repeat, onion ring searing my tongue. "Don't make him do something he hates."

Our father shrugs and plants a hand on my shoulder. His eyes are the kind of blue that read unnatural—like he's downed a liter of anti-freeze.

I realize that before her nap, our mother had taken some of her new anti-anxiety med. Now, she slumps over herself as she eats, black eyes unfocused, her plate sagging so that her onion rings tumble to the earth.

Our father tries to engage her, "Why don't we all hang out by the beach tonight and roast s'mores? Doesn't that sound nice? You can tell that Korean ghost story your mother always told you. The kids haven't heard that one in a while," but she's elsewhere.

Our mother used to tell lots of stories, about her mother, about her dreams of Korea, about old boyfriends and growing up in Junction City. Grain by grain, her joy was exchanged with violence, her openness with feeling that every person and every question was a challenge to her validity. In place of her joy, anger collects in her veins, builds, builds, builds, until she can't hold it anymore. Her words have always been her best weapon. The vivacity with which she can dismantle your selfworth in two sentences, flake away at the wallpaper of your resolve until she turns you in her favor. The way she talks about "skinning your arms," you're being so bad. She's done it before, in middle school, to some bitch who called her a gook. Her less-sour state has appeared over the last few months; a new cocktail of anti-anxiety and sleeping and pain pills (to treat her once-broken back) do the work that she could not. Dampening the rage (sadness, regret) most of the time.

Even though I know I should stay with Chung, bear out the boredom and the long game our father is playing, I can't stay another second. My limbs burn.

"I'm going on a walk," I say, leaving the campsite, not looking back, following a trail deep into the woods.

The sky feels long in the way it does before sunset. The colors, the tired stretch of the light. Alone, I feel myself returning, as if being in their presence, being around our parents, strips away some vital element in me. I march through the brush and overturned logs as if I am a knight. I take up a sword and slash away mosquitoes. Beat the trunks of twisted, diseased trees and dream of immense political dramas, or a damsel I would swoop in and save at the last minute and marry in an open-air simple wedding. Not very ladylike, my mother would say in her more sober moments. But I could stay in the woods, at the lake, I think. I would be happy.

Time slips away, and the light fades. It's another nearly moonless night and I know I should head back, not because our parents will worry, not because I would be missed, but out of duty. I find a smooth patch of pre-arranged limestone, an in-woods campsite for the more daring, far into the woods, and lie back. The trees shake and boom in the wind, mammoth.

I close my eyes, breathe in the woody air so deep I feel it settle there, in the deepest of the deep of me.

The wind stills for a moment, and I hear crunching leaves and tossing brush to my left. I sit up, paranoid, dreaming of the worst monster imaginable. A man carrying a small homemade lantern stumbles into the campsite. He walks over to what I now see is an established dwelling, a well-crafted shack of fallen logs, woven together and covered by a tarp. He doubles back when he sees me. I wave. He waves back and smiles.

The man is hairy, head hairy, chin-and-neck hairy. His coat is old blue and covered in dirt and sweat stains, and from where I sit, he looks like he's been wearing the same jeans since he was a teen, however many decades ago.

I stand up and pat dust off my shorts. "I'm sorry," I say. "I couldn't see anything. I didn't realize—."

He bears a toothless grin and waves my words away.

"Do you live here?" I ask.

He nods. He lights a fire in the small, tin-outlined pit, and I see the space more fully. A rusted-out bike, many bottles, cans, and emptied processed-food containers scatter across the earth. The man sits and invites me to rest again, so I do.

"Is it nice here? I think I want to live here, in the woods."

When I settle, he scratches his throat and stretches his jaw before he speaks. His voice rasps, like he hasn't spoken to someone in months or maybe years.

"Nice," he says. "It stinks."

This makes me laugh, and I think I would have a nice friend out here, if I ditched the farm and made my home here. The wind winds through the trees and blows the fire wayward; the smoke comes up into my lungs and eyes and I have to move.

"I'm sorry, I should probably leave anyway. Thanks for letting me stay."

The man nods and grins, hunching over his knees. As I trek into the black, he whistles. I look back to see him holding something out to me, an old floatie in the shape of an orca, paled by sun exposure.

I trudge back to my father's campsite holding it over my head, the spoils of my expedition. In the vague lights outlining the trees, I find my way. When I return, our parents are in the RV, and my ears pick up a hum, a sound that means revived anger. Chung sits near the water. As I come up to the shore, I see he's building shapes out of the sand.

"Castle?" I ask.

"Silos."

"Creative," I say.

"Where were you?" His voice comes out raw.

I show him the floatie.

"Where did you get this?"

"A man in the woods."

"You're lying. It's gross. It smells."

"Everything smells. I think it's cool."

Our parents resurface from the trailer. I was wrong about the anger, it seems, because along with the parents comes a couple I've never seen before. They gather around the fire. When our father realizes I've returned, he waves me over.

The couple is older. The wife is slender with silver-brown hair and green eyes and wears a patchy dress that reaches real low on her chest, exposing the concaves of her sternum. The husband is tan with long, stringy hair and shallow-set wandering eyes. They ask me about school and books and boys. Then our parents and the couple talk lake-things—fishing, boating, cliff diving.

Our father has crazy stories from his youth, cliff diving with his cousin a hundred feet up, close brushes with spear-like rocks.

They drink, the couple. They start to offer our parents beers, but our mother ends their sentence with an abrupt, "No." Her most lucid moment of the trip.

I tell Chung we should set up the tent, and once we do, I read to him for half an hour before we both fade quickly into sleep.

AROUND midnight, I wake to that hum, that familiar hum, of far-off but not-far-enough-off anger. I exit the tent. Stumble in my half-awake daze over the rough ground, eyes focusing on the four figures dancing around the still-roiling fire.

"Stop it." Chung follows me, whining deep in his throat, fingers to lips. "Stop!" he screams, circling them, the water licking his feet.

In their shifting they knock him down into the waves. I cut the bottoms of my feet on broken glass. Our father breaks free, digs his hand into the fire and throws a glowing rock at our mother's face. He sprints. Up the hill. Toward the cliffs. He's faster than I've ever seen him before.

Our mother ignores her burn. Turns. Strains to keep up with him, black hair a veil cast against the sky. She doesn't catch up in time.

He flies.

And she collapses—from exhaustion, from despair—on the harsh rock. Cries or yells. More emotion than she's shown in days, weeks, months.

Seconds (that feel like hours) later, Chung and I spot red-and-blue lights squirm into the horizon, wriggle across the black. The couple called the cops the moment our parents started shouting. The lights form a familiar beacon, of peace to come, of apologies and reconciliations.

I won't go back. I pray to the earth, *Please, swallow up the police cars, keep the chaos just a little longer. This time around they can't forgive each other. They'll abandon the charade for good. Please, please, please release us.*

The land hears my prayer but denies my plea.

Instead, I realize Chung is not beside me. He's nowhere on the beach or in the tent or line of trees. I scour the darkness. Call out his name.

Then I spy a faint, gray speck in the distance, bobbing to the rhythm of the lake. A flash of neon blue against the black, Chung's little arms raised for the sky.

I plunge into the waters, paddle and inhale water and feel fish slide against my ankles.

I find him drifting on the inflated orca, reaching towards me.

"Come on," his eyes brim with hope, like he's setting off on a long journey, and I know that he has prayed the same as I have. That he is ready to be free, too. "Come with me."

I pause, look to the shore and the fractious black. Our parents handcuffed. Our course correcting. I know my weight will sink us. As I jump on, a pulling comes. Whirlpool sucking down.

THIS *is it,*
this is it,
this is it.
The water fell all around them.

The Color of Fear

The Brother

THE COLOR OF FEAR

GREEN—PURPLE—ORANGE. It's the water. The sliver of moon obscured by the lake, so far from him now. Chung's art teacher will teach his class secondary colors (two years from now), but Chung knows the truth from this moment onward. It is the thick ring of iris around a carp's pupil as it swims parallel to him—follows him as he drops lower, closer to the earth's heart. Orange, the color of the sun as it greets him each sleepless morning. Purple, the bags under his eyes. Green, the color of his sister's irises when she cries, whenever she grows angry (their permanent color if she and he survive this moment). Green are the weeds that wrap his ankles. Purple, the color of his fear. Orange is the hand that seizes him, but not before he hears something. A voice. It offers a message, but his brain fails him. Later, he searches his memory for a word, a command received, but all he recalls is the feeling—of being cleaved—and the sound—from which no human or animal origin can be named. Like a hiss. Like a moan. Like a trill. But the hand jerks him and the air returns to him, though ponderous—and the slog back to shore will be long and cold and hard, so long and cold and hard that the voice and its message will become relics, lost to the water. It takes twenty years for it to call to him again, and only then is the brother ready to listen.

Churn

Another

CHURN

THE brother and sister sank to the bottom of the lake, pulled by some unexpected current. As they drifted farther from the surface, the sister closed her eyes, surprised by her lack of urgency, her willingness to dissolve into that vile lake rather than return to their mother and father. They dropped ten, twenty feet before she opened her eyes and saw the brother, all open-mouth-and-flitting-eyelids, laid out next to her like a ragdoll. But just as the lake's silty bottom gave against her feet, she gained the energy (that last-minute clarity) to grab her little brother and propel them upwards, away from that resting place, away from peace, and back into the flashy realm of the living.

Red-and-blue lights punctuated the black shore. Their parents were already cuffed, already being treated by medics: a burnt strip of cheek for the mother, a broken wrist and dislocated shoulder for the father. It was clear as the sister and the brother crept into that light, that multi-colored parade, that none had known of the children's existence. Their parents had been too incapacitated to remember them. A brassy-eyed cop turned to face them, stunned, still holding the notebook that marked each childish violent act that had led to their parents' fight.

Their mother would spend the rest of her night in the county jail; their father's was spent in the hospital. Their grandparents (their father's parents) showed up at one thirty in the morning to take the children home. On the drive back, which was just over an hour, neither their grandmother nor grandfather would say anything of significance; they had given up soothing their grandchildren years ago when these late-night rescues had been less frequent.

Their grandfather's pickup hadn't crawled back onto their farm's gravel driveway until nearly three. All the sounds that the farm's many sheds and open fields and not-so-distant creeks bred—the brother couldn't remember ever hearing them, ever being awake so late that their cacophony pricked him, kept his senses alert. He didn't sleep until many hours later (not so many hours before their grandparents woke them with offerings of eggs and bacon and orange juice); he felt sick-to-his-stomach at the smell. Felt a burning in his skull at the early sun. A ringing in his ears at the shushed voices of his grandmother and grandfather.

Had their paternal grandparents not been the German-blooded kind of farmers who rose at dawn every day, perhaps the children could have stayed home from school that day. Slept in. But no, there were knocks on each of their bedroom doors soon after the sun set the prairie in motion. Both siblings liked to imagine their *maternal* grandmother, who had come from Korea, would have been the kind to let them sleep late and sit on her lap and say how much she loved them, but they would never know because she died before they were born.

After the knock at the door, the sister in her bed, who'd been deep in a black, dreamless sleep, stirred to her brother whimpering from the other room, an utterance he often made without recognizing it. She showered because she still stunk of the lake. Felt its skin on her skin. She ate the breakfast her grandparents made and wondered how, with all their clanking pans and the fresh scents of the food, she hadn't woken earlier. She usually slept shallowly, waking up five, six times a night.

Full and cleaned and rested, she sat on the farmhouse porch, on the rusted swing her grandparents had hung fifteen years ago when they still lived here, before they gifted this house and all its land to her parents. She tried thinking of the night before. The depths she and her brother had traveled. The weight of all the lake above them. Her mind frenzied, scattered its details so that she couldn't make sense of it. She stayed there, spying a storm creeping from the west—the same one that had dotted the shore of the lake before she swam after her brother—until the yellow school bus made its turn, a half-a-mile up, and her brother shuffled out the door looking so gray.

Their grandparents didn't say goodbye as the children met the bus, boarded against its sulfuric belch, and found their usual seats. Normal life roared back around them, all pinched arms and carved insults and ripe body odor and metallic braces spitting promises of the day.

The children's school was the kind to be in the middle of a cow pasture, to house students from kindergarten through high school in one large labyrinthine building. At the entry the sister watched her little brother exit into the lower-elementary hallway. She wove through the crowd of children to her locker, which was at the very end by a double-door exit looking on to a path leading down to the football field.

A girl appeared behind the doors, all black hair and long legs spanning out from dress-code-breaking shorts. The girl rattled the door handles. Locked out.

Instantly, the girl's eyes landed on the sister. She lifted up her hands. *Well?*

As the sister opened the door, she smelled a rush of something thick and acidic that reminded her of her mother.

"Thanks," the girl said.

It was impossible not to know everyone by name in this tiny school, and so the sister knew the nameless girl to be new, and because it was March, knew that meant the girl's family had either moved here in a rush or that the girl had been removed from her previous school *(for punishment? for her safety?)*. Watching the girl punch her knuckles against the lockers as she marched down the hallway, the sister guessed she had been kicked out. Maybe from one of those Salina schools, giant (or seemingly giant) and always sending their maladjusted to rough it in the country.

When the sister arrived at her first class, she saw that the girl had taken her desk, the sister's desk (she'd fought hard for that spot) right by the window and at the back of the room. She had never been the kind of person to confront someone, but she felt a heat press into her chest, her cheeks, and approached the desk from the side.

"That's actually *my* desk," she said, pointing at the name card on the side of it.

"Jordan," the nameless girl read. "Isn't that a boy's name?"

When the sister didn't respond the girl leaned back in the chair and kicked up her feet; she wore white Nikes with *fuego bitch* scrawled on the sides.

"Well, I can share," she said, though her shoes claimed the expanse.

The sister felt oddly threatened, scrutinized by the girl. Still, that flush in her chest and face roared and her ears hummed. She wanted to call her a bitch, but that wouldn't do any good. She wanted to shove those feet off the desk. All that chaos, all that filth she had endured the day before, and now this? A ripple crept across her stomach and she was just about to act, she didn't know how, when her teacher entered the room and told the new girl to come to the front of the class.

The sister took her desk back, rubbing the girl's dirt off its surface.

"This is Amy Badillo," the teacher announced. "Please make her feel welcome."

ALL morning, the brother's senses refused to settle. He had never slept so little, at least that he could remember. If losing sleep meant that everything in the world doubled, he decided he would rather sleep for days than have to miss a few hours' sleep again.

In math class his teacher passed out the minute-long timetables they practiced every week. A minute and all those numbers to rack up. For fifty-five seconds he stared at the white paper, the black glyphs. In his last five seconds he answered three; not enough to pass, to add up to anything at all. As his teacher collected their work, she stopped at his desk. Maybe she noticed his bloodshot eyes or the slight tremble to his hand. Maybe she noticed nothing at all, as usual. But the paper, she held it aloft for too long.

"Not good," she said to the paper and continued on down the line.

"Not good," a fat-nosed blonde with tiny fists mimicked. "Not good. Not good."

Becky L. and Jesse M. and Alexes A. and B. laughed.

The brother wanted to laugh too, because it was funny, how easily he had failed, but the sound dropped lower into his throat, heavy, until his stomach was rattling—his throat hot and his mouth all saliva—and he was rushing to the bathroom, but instead of the privacy of a stall, instead of the cool of the bathroom tile on his knees and the porcelain on his palms, he lost it in the hallway. Egg and bacon and orange juice, on the floor, on his chin, eating holes in his throat, edging away at his teeth. It got on his shoes and legs and a little on his shorts (which were denim and would carry the stench all day long), so after, he did run on to the bathroom to kneel in a stall (he had more to give up, much more), and gagging from the smell of Clorox and

- 18 -

splashed pattern of others' botched arrivals he waited until everything had been emptied out. He flushed, wiped his mouth on toilet paper, its fibers caked at the corners of his lips; he was washing his hands when the janitor came in. The brother couldn't look at him.

"Go to the nurse," the janitor said, and he did, all guilt and relief and impatience, because the day was so long and already making a target of him.

AT first recess, which was shared between second, fifth, and sixth graders, the sister climbed to the top of the monkey bars, something she was often too scared to attempt, but today she couldn't take her eyes off the sky. The storm and its gravity had arrived. Low clouds skirted by, bound for somewhere east, and teal behemoths stalled above them. It was at the first crack of lightning and spit of thunder that the teachers' whistles blew. The sister heard the clap of her classmates' feet against the asphalt, heading indoors, but she wasn't ready to leave just yet.

Still, the night before blurred. She remembered the kiss of the lake's belly, the might, the propulsion it had taken for her to hoist her brother to the surface, to swim them to shore. She remembered the pat of rain, the shuddering of thunder, the tremoring call of the woods, but she felt somewhere in these recollections a loss. A missed beat

No one noticed her, still flattened against the monkey bars, and so she stayed there, greeting this ominous gathering of atmosphere until the rain grew to dollops and the air ripened to emerald.

She sprinted inside, soaked, and toweled off in the junior high girls' locker room, which she had often snuck into during past emergencies, years before it was hers to claim. In the hallway leading back to the upper-elementary school wing, she made room for the janitor (who rolled his mop bucket at a snail's pace), and passed the principal's office, which she had only visited once—when her father had gotten into a four-wheeler accident (one of many), and was being taken to the hospital.

Back in her classroom the sister saw Amy, the new girl, lounging at her desk again, this time with her bare feet on the slick particleboard surface. The teacher hadn't noticed—Reading Period—she was in her own world. Again a ripple cast across the sister's stomach and she thought of all the ways she could hurt this girl, make her feel small, unwanted, things she had rarely considered doing before, but, once again, she was robbed of her chance.

The school intercom stuttered on. The principal said that the National Weather Service had just issued a tornado warning for the county. Everyone needed to head to the lower tunnel, which wrapped around the basketball court and was constructed of concrete. Already, the high whirr of sirens crept into the school, blaring all across Salina and audible even here, six miles out.

As the seven hundred-odd kids and preteens and teenagers filed through the many hallways to their singular shelter, the sister spied her brother in the crowd (still pallid, despite his dark skin, and looking feverish), now wearing different clothes. If they hadn't been the only part-Korean students in the whole school, she might've thought he was another boy.

She thought to chase after him, ride out the storm with him, but he was out of view before she could get close.

WHEN his shorts had been changed and shoes wiped clean, the nurse took the brother's temperature. Ninety-six degrees. She took his blood pressure and gave him a small cup of Pepto-Bismol, which coated his mouth and tasted horrible. The nurse said he could rest in the curtained bed at the back of her office until lunchtime, but the sirens and the principal's voice boomed over him before then.

In the tunnel the brother crouched shoulder-to-shoulder with the small-fisted boy and big-mouthed Becky L. The concrete corridor was used for storage when it wasn't stuffed with children and preteens and teenagers, and so across from him in the narrow space sat forgotten chairs and broken tables and a life-sized cutout of Daren the Lion, an anti-drug mascot. Even here, they could hear the storm's strength grow. The flimsy roof of the basketball court creaked under the wind, and it sounded as though hail punctured the cheap material. Even from the tunnel, this noise pressed in on them. The brother's senses still overreacted, each sound sending a pulse of pain through his head.

"Dung," the small-fisted boy called straight into the brother's right ear. "Seriously, why would your mom name you something that rhymes with Dung? Does she hate you?"

The brother swallowed, feeling nausea roll down the sides of his mouth. *Maybe,* he wanted to respond. When she wasn't rendered catatonic by her meds, she was always trying to rope him into her fights with his father, his grandparents, his sister. His mother had been the one to name him.

She'd never learned Korean from her mother (her mother wouldn't teach her), and so his mother had found the name in an international baby-names book: Chung. She had been robbed the right to name his sister (who was named after their father's brother who died when he was five), and she probably hadn't considered the way his name would catch in people's throats, make him even more of a target than his dark hair and skin did. His sister had the white name and the white skin and had never been sent to the principal like he had (over untied shoes or someone's misplaced lunch box or an inability to stop crying).

"Did you hear me?" the big-fisted boy jabbed. "I asked if your mom hates you."

Even in the tunnel, they could hear the tornado sirens from Salina. That, or the brother was so sleep deprived he imagined them. He wished the tornado would come. He hadn't wanted to escape the lake. Not that he wanted to die. The opposite. He wanted freedom. He wanted a new family with fresh faces and a quieter home and a school that didn't smell like cow pies.

The small-fisted boy punched his arm, though not very hard because he was weak. "Talk to me," the kid said, as if the brother and he were friends, as if the brother was beholden to his questions. The kid punched his arm again and, over time, the punches began to hurt.

Still, the brother didn't respond. He didn't know how.

So the boy slapped his arm, *clap clap clap,* until a teacher stood, ten kids down, and started wading over to them.

The brother tried to look normal. Play it cool. But before the teacher could reach them, a murmur of voices rose, swelled to cries.

"Fire!" one kid yelled, and so the others followed.

THE sister didn't know how it happened. How in all her avoiding the new girl, she still wound up kneeling across from her in the concrete tunnel not meant to hold seven hundred children and teachers. The tunnel reeked, not just from the built-up moisture and defunct equipment but from all the sweaty bodies, too.

The new girl smiled, her knees knocking the sisters'.

Why the girl cared about her, the sister didn't know. Why the girl had singled her out, why she had chosen this day to antagonize her. It was too much. The sister knotted her fists, let them turn white. She had never wanted to punch someone until today.

"Do you want to know why I'm here?" the new girl asked, unfurling her own fists.

"I do," the sister said, vibrating with an anger she could usually stamp out.

But the new girl paused, dug dirt from one of her fingernails.

"You beat someone up and got kicked out," the sister guessed.

The new girl laughed, too low-pitched for a sixth grader. "No." She drew invisible lines on her face. "Some bitch got her teeth knocked out for calling me a jap."

The sister looked over the girl.

"I'm not even Asian!" the girl said, spreading her palms wide, arms high. "My dad's from Guatemala."

And the sister understood. Greasy, limp-haired boys or men were always "confused" by her little brother's looks. He had been called anti-Mexican slurs more than anything else (always behind his back, always directed at their buddies or other popular guys, so that the sister couldn't confront them without admitting she was eavesdropping).

"If you didn't beat her up, who did?" the sister asked, curious now.

"The pavement." The new girl smiled, and the sister laughed.

The hail and the wind and the rain brought them a familiar song through the tunnel doors. Tornadoes were ordinary in central Kansas. The sister and her father would sit on their front porch and watch them twist across the horizon. Once or twice, the whole family crammed into their pickup and chased after, keeping a few miles' distance, until it changed course and wound up speeding away, sending gravel high and into fields. One time, three pencil-thin tornadoes had slowly convened, formed an F3 that leveled a family friend's home. He was fine, but two dozen of his cattle got swept away, and he ended up moving to town rather than rebuilding.

"So, you're from Salina," the sister said.

"No. My dad owns a farm over by Gypsum."

Gypsum was only six miles from the sister's farm. How had she never seen this girl before? All the farmers in Saline County knew each other.

"Wheat and milo and soybean and corn and alfalfa," the new girl said.

"Same," the sister said, though her family's crops had dwindled to nothing over the last few years. She was just about to ask the new girl why her parents hadn't had her go to school here all along, here where all the farmer's kids went, when Max M., one of the greasy, limp-haired boys she'd heard call her brother a slur before, sidled in next to the new girl to try his damp hand at flirting.

"What'd you get in trouble for to get stuck in this craphole?"

The sister's shuddering stomach returned. Sweat rolled over her skin and she found that irrepressible anger sparking up her throat again. "How old are you?" she said. He was two grades above them.

"Why don't we get out of here?" he whispered to the new girl.

The sister clenched her fists again. Maybe it was the proximity, the lack of airflow. She felt sick. She felt incendiary. "We're not interested," she said, ignoring the boy's thigh pressed against hers. "Bother someone in your own grade."

He barely registered her, had his eyes on the new girl, whose gaze bore at the sister's stomach. Could she sense what was happening to her?

"I included you out of courtesy," the older boy said, finally pointing his nose at her. His breath stank of death. Like the lake. Like the farm. "*You're not even pretty.*"

One second she was an ordinary, not-even-pretty, preteen girl. The next, a geyser. A disturbance. She didn't put it together until it happened. That all day—ever since the night before when she had given all she had to pull herself and her little brother from the lake's grip, to do what her parents could not—something new and toxic and formidable had been cooking inside her. Ashy and resembling burnt wood, a cloud of smoke billowed out of her mouth and nose.

At first she couldn't move, couldn't stop the thing from filling the entirety of the tunnel with her cinders. One kid yelled "fire" and the rest followed. A stampede, seven hundred kids scrambling out of the tight space.

Then the sister's eruption ended as soon as it began and she rushed through the basketball court along with everyone else. She kept running, tracing through the hallways, desperate to get outdoors before it could come again.

Outside, she was alone. It had stopped raining, though a light spray swept from the roof onto the grass leading down to the football field. The sky retained its greenish hue, and the already-melting hail made a checkerboard of the lawn.

The fresh air gave her time to process what had happened. The taste of the smoke, earthy, stayed on her tongue, and her throat burned, but only a little, like her body was just getting adjusted, forming calluses before more burns could come. She rested against the cool brick of the building and regulated her breath. Still, she could feel a disturbance inside her deciding whether to make a rise again. As she waited for its return, the sister watched the sky, the blanketed horizon. From a hook in the clouds a mass began to form. Coiling, tempered. Every second gaining more ground.

THE brother followed the crowd, which convened in the cafeteria, then the parking lot, as the teachers inspected the tunnel. The sirens from Salina had stopped, but any Kansan worth their salt would've seen that they weren't past danger yet. The clouds stalled. The rain, which had taken a break, was puttering back into gear.

"Hey!" the brother heard from his left. He had wound up in a group of teenagers and so his view was obscured. "Hey!" the voice called again, getting closer. From around a football players' wide hips the blonde small-fisted boy ran at him. "Why don't you like me?" the kid said as he hit his powerless little fists on the brother's chest. On his face.

The brother ended up on the ground, not from the boy but from knocking into a high schooler's back and the reflexive elbow jerk that followed.

"Why don't you like me?" the boy yelled, hysterical and pounding all over him now—he, a caught fish, wide eyes and open mouth.

Another high-schooler jock pulled the kid off. A teacher rushed over. Grabbed both grade-school boys by the collar of their shirts. Even with all the hits he took the brother wasn't bloodied, his skin hadn't ballooned at all. It was the other kid whose knuckles had split and whose face waxed red.

The tunnel was cleared. The smoke chalked up to some mischievous kids who had lit a cardboard cut-out (though no evidence was found). Then everyone was ushered back in there again because the danger of ripped roofs and shattered windows still loomed. And the two boys were carried to the very end of the snaking line, where the principal waited for them.

"You're not making a good case for yourself, are you?" he said to the brother. "What did he do to deserve you making him bleed? You don't want to be here, do you?

And though the brother wanted to answer, "*No, I really don't, I want to sink back, return to the lake, to anywhere but here*"—he didn't. He took the principal's words and hard looks and stuffed them down, pressing deep into the pit of his stomach until, without knowing how, without a thought for crying *"help"* or reaching for steadier arms, he dropped. Went black. Felt the hard scrape of the concrete on his elbow and the side of his knee as his limbs wriggled, neck straightened.

Later, they would say his eyes were lidless—blank—but all he would remember was the shiftless black. The stench of still water. The burn of his lungs gasping for air no longer meant for him.

*W*HEN the tornado finally hit ground, the sister had reached an understanding. *Keep your cool and we won't have any problems,* said the fire down her throat. This had never been a problem for her before, but maybe the lake had changed her chemistry, made her more flammable. She wouldn't know until new threats arrived.

The double-doors clicked open. The new girl stepped out. It was raining again, and both girls pancaked themselves against the wall to keep dry. The new girl spied for the first time the tornado, five miles off, carving up someone's crops or barn or maybe just an old, abandoned house no one had cared about for decades.

"Should we tell someone?" the girl asked.

"What would they be able to do?" the sister replied, smelling again that harsh acid emanating from the girl next to her.

"I meant about your—. You know. " She tilted her head at her.

"I know," the sister said.

The new girl pulled out a red-lined pack. Marlboros. The same the sister's mother smoked. "Well, if it's worth anything," she took a long drag like she had been doing this all her life, "I think it's pretty cool." She held out the plastic-wrapped pack. "I'd give all of these to have that kind of power."

And the sister nodded because the girl, Amy, wasn't wrong. Even if the sister's parents returned and their fighting resumed and nobody learned anything and their farm stayed dying and her classmates stayed assholes, at least she had one thing that was hers—that no one could claim wasn't remarkable. It was born from something stronger than them, than all of them, and if she just held tight, eventually she would be someone worth running from.

Someone worth fearing.

Godless

The Sister

GODLESS

FARM girls are granted a high distinction in Kansas. You know the country. Your blood (or if not yours, your ancestors') has poured into the soil. Pious, my family has made substantial sacrifice over our four decades on this farm. A young boy (my uncle) and three of my unborn siblings, all come into this world through so much pain. Dozens of cats, six or seven dogs, and fifty calves have died in my lifetime alone. If you were godless once, you became reverent by necessity, not to a heavenly god but to the earth. So, as our mother boxes up our favorite stuffed animals and our best pots and pans and our few remaining heirlooms, I begin to grieve. A loss of home, a loss of distinction, a loss of god.

Chung howls as our mother makes us load boxes into the van. "No," he cries, echoed by nearby coyotes, "I don't want to go."

I know better than to argue. I help our mother with a cumbrous box of dishes and silverware, and though my arms shake and sweat pools below my eyes and the heat is triple digits, I don't say anything when she pauses to scold Chung.

"If you'd rather stay, then stay here by yourself. Your daddy will be back in five weeks. I'm sure you'll survive until then," she cackles. She loves to offer us freedoms she knows we won't take.

Our father has been booked into a six-week rehab program in Atchison just last week. Our mother barely waits a day before she starts packing.

After Chung shoves the boxes into the backseat, I make him help me with the mattress. We can only fit one. We choose mine. A full bed, more than enough for Chung and me to share. At ten, he's framed like a limp Pinocchio, strings holding him together. I'm nearing thirteen, and though my mother prefers to call me "stalky," I'm the shortest and lightest in my class.

Because Chung and I are lighter than flyweights it takes time to haul the mattress from my bedroom at the back of the hallway, through the crooked foot-space of the living room where our TV and Nintendo 64 will stay, past the dining room with our great-grandmother's dining table and chairs, and the kitchen that our mother has all but emptied. Twice Chung needs to stop, set the mattress down, catch his breath. All that time I hear our mother from the front porch, cooing to the cats we're about to abandon. All that time, my biceps tremble and my elbows begin to ache.

"Let's go," I keep saying, even though I can see he's about to lock up, freeze, go flat.

Just before we come to the front door, Chung's lips stretch, contort, and his eyes lid over.

Three months ago, Chung suddenly developed seizures. We called them seizures. Really, our mutual near-death experience in the bed of a rotting lake had mutated both of us. A fire grows inside me. It never dies, even as I hold my breath as long as I can, trying to deprive it of oxygen. And Chung? He can't stand our parents' arguments anymore. Stops breathing, writhes like a maniac until they stop. This, I assume, was the last nail in the coffin of their marriage. The reason for our move.

"Come on, it's okay," I soothe him. "We're almost there. It'll be alright."

"I don't want to go."

We get to the front porch, down the four steps, and then he loses it. He doesn't drop the mattress, but he stops in his steps, adolescent cats, limber, snaking between his legs.

"No," he wails again, and this time he can't control it. His arms begin to shake.

Our mother, bending to pet one of the mother cats, looks in our direction. "What is taking so long? We need to go."

I try to get his attention, to lock eyes, but Chung is gone, irretrievable behind his frenzy. I can feel my arms going numb holding all the weight, joints flaming, the rib-dented bellies of cats pressing against my calves—the July summer unforgiving, the land unforgiving, cold, already shuttering itself away from me.

I drop the mattress. Chung forfeits his half. And just like that, I become soft. Not a tough country girl, not a farm girl, as I watch the mattress descend onto the grass, onto the cat-shit-spotted yard, a flurry of paws and peaked tails rushing for safety. Our mother—she can't say a thing—only gapes from her place among them.

SHE'S found a two-bedroom loft apartment in Salina that has a pool and a laundry room and a decent landlord.

For a third time today, Chung and I carry a mattress, this time up the short flight of stairs leading to our new apartment, and up the double-long stairs to the loft that will become Chung's "bedroom." Because my full-sized mattress is ruined we have taken Chung's twin bed from the farm, which he will sleep on alone, no box spring, no frame, laid across flattened carpet that smells like our old milk barn after a decade of abandonment.

As my limbs tremble and joints ache, I try to remember that our mother hasn't left the moving to us by choice. That her years of Tae Kwon Do and our troubled births have made lifting almost anything impossible for her.

After we deposit the mattress, Chung and I pause, secret, in the apartment. Cool down. We take turns fanning the refrigerator door for each other. Catching our breaths.

Outside, we find our mother talking to someone we assume to be our neighbor. A mountain lion of a man. He's black-eyed, thin-lipped, and beautifully blonde.

"Kent," our mother says in a voice so rarely used we forget she's our mother for a moment. "This is Jordan, Chung. We just moved from the country," and she says this last word like a curse. The country, where bumpkins, unlike us, unlike her, live. Even without knowing him, I can tell he has never lived off this land.

Kent says nothing to Chung and me. He nods, yes, but doesn't speak to us. He and our mother discuss employment opportunities in town, which are apparently numerous for a bright young woman like our mother.

Chung and I celebrate the deposit of the final boxes into the apartment by rubbing ice cubes over each other's faces and arms. Chung shivers, gleeful, with each swipe of that cool bliss. He's forgotten his frenzy, forgotten the farm already, and a part of me is relieved, a part of me envious.

That night our mother sleeps on a pile of clothes. I sleep on another twin mattress that Kent hauled over when he learned of our scarcity.

My bedroom, which is an eight-by-eight-foot square, blocked off by a sliding room divider, is dense with heat and the musk of mildew. I can't sleep. I can't cry. I think of the cats, their loneliness, and that alone should make me cry. They are my best friends, sometimes my only friends. I helped birth them, have wandered through the farm to locate them when their mothers hide them away—in a maze of hay bales, in just-open tractor cabins, on the smooth cool tops of garage doors that once fallen were never moved from their horizontal position. I can't cry. I think of our uncle, who died so young on that farm, run over by a tractor when he was five years old. His ghost so lonely.

And still, I cannot cry.

ANNOYED, sapped (I'm guessing), our mother decides in our second week at the new apartment that I'm too much to deal with. "Short-tempered," she calls me, which isn't wrong. She calls Molly Rohr's mother and convinces her to have me over for a night. I don't protest. I like Molly. I don't like her brother. I like their little town, too, just below four hundred people. No gas station, one convenience store, and one church. Gypsum is one of a few smaller towns in Saline County that pale against Salina's literal glow. Fifty-thousand people means Salina isn't a town to us. It's a city.

Molly, Matt, and their parents live in a two-story house off of Main Street, the only paved road in town. Their driveway is gravel, a delight, as I have begun to choke on the fumes of asphalt, the claustrophobia of narrow city streets. As my mother pulls up in the van and onto the gravel, I feel a shift. Like a homecoming.

Molly's mother, a walking, talking Mama Bear Berenstain-turned-human, wraps her arms around me as I shuffle toward their front door, desperate for air conditioning. (Our mother never runs the air conditioning in the van. It's a waste of gas.) Mrs. Rohr takes me in the first hug I've had in months. Maybe a year. I should appreciate it more, recharge, but I'm desperate to be cool, to be indoors.

Inside, I find Matt sitting legs splayed, gym shorts hiked up, Mountain Dew in hand, at the foot of the stairs leading up to Molly's bedroom. He sees me before I see him. He's grinning, holding his pop can out to me. He's fifteen, about to go into high school because he was held back in first grade.

"Have a sip?" he asks.

"No thanks."

As I approach the stairs, backpack in hand, he doesn't move. He keeps grinning, keeps his hand outstretched. "Have a sip," he says again.

"No thanks." I move to climb the stairs, knee knocking into his, but he scoots to block me.

"Come on. You've gotta be thirsty. It's balls-hot out there."

I take the can from him, careful to avoid his hands, which I know from experience will be sticky, sweaty, and take the smallest sip of Mountain Dew. It's down my throat before I realize it's off. It burns me. I choke and choke, and he laughs.

"Mountain Man Screw."

"What?" I ask, wishing the taste out of my mouth.

"I call it Mountain Man Screw. Mountain Dew, orange juice, whiskey."

"That's disgusting," I say, and I push past him as hard as I can. He doesn't move out of my way, so my knee rams his shoulder as I pass.

I find Molly leaning against her window, staring out into the street, her shorts rolled up so high you can see every inch of her thighs and her bra straps fallen over her shoulders. Her tank top ripped and tied into a dozen knots. When she sees me, she calls me over, pointing toward the window.

"John Wesley is mowing the lawn! Come look."

And she's right. There's John Wesley, a class ahead of us, shirtless and pushing a mower that's surely coated in his sweat by now. You could call him handsome, but I choose not to. He is the kind to delight in wearing a cowboy hat and snake-skin boots. To love country music. He's the type to never leave here, small-town Kansas, but never live off the land, either.

"He is," I say. I ask her how her summer has been, but she doesn't answer. Instead, she takes my hand and leads me out of the room, down the stairs as her brother moves out of the way, and out into the terrible heat once again.

"Hey! Hey, Pretty Boy!" Molly takes us across the street without looking both ways. She has to scream because the lawn mower roars and sputters.

It takes her three tries before John finally notices her hand-to-hip on his freshly trimmed lawn, me curling into myself, uncomfortable, hot, wishing to be indoors. He doesn't grin. He's half-a-foot taller than me, just above Molly's height. He slams the mower off and comes up to us, and I think Molly is going to punch him she's standing so erect.

"Hey, you are going to meet Jordan and me right here. Tonight. 9 p.m."

His face doesn't change. Looks down at us, wipes his hands on his shirt.

"I'm doing what?" John asks.

"You heard me. 9. Don't be late."

Inside the house, she laughs like she has to get all the air out of her lungs at once. She digs her hands into her thighs, bends as if to puke, and laughs, laughs, laughs. This is what I like about Molly. She sees what she wants and acts on it. She has little capacity to lie, to deceive. I convince myself I could be like her with enough practice.

For dinner, Mrs. Rohr prepares us fried chicken and potatoes and sweet corn. It's delicious. She gifts each of us children a chilled glass of strawberry milk after our meal.

"We are so happy to have you," she tells me as I rinse my plate in the kitchen.

Another day and I may hate her for her warmth. Instead, I thank her.

"I need more good little girls like you around," she says. "Molly needs a friend like you."

I thank her again. On my way to rejoin the rest of the Rohrs, I shove a silly smile from my face. *Be cool, Jordan. This is not where you belong.*

JOHN meets us at exactly nine. He's in a well-fitted white T-shirt, washed jeans tighter than boot cut. His cleanliness surprises me.

He lets Molly lead him away from the trim lawn, onto one of the gravel roads spanning away from the main artery of Gypsum. We're two houses away from the Rohr's when I hear heavy breathing, footsteps coming from behind. We look back to see Matt, still in his gym shorts, carrying two Mountain Dews that slosh over his knuckles as he jogs.

"Go away," Molly says.

"Jordan invited me," he says, and before I can reply that I didn't, he's by my side, trying to offer me another Mountain Man Screw.

I can smell the alcohol this time. I feel like vomiting. Molly tells him again and again, "go home," but he keeps apace with us. She leads us to the most predictable place for trackless teens to go late at night. The old K-12 school, all brick, windows half smashed, weeds sprouting through the long-cracked flooring. They had already built a new school out in the country when this one was hit by an F-4 tornado that decimated half the town twenty years back. Molly guides us through a moonlit hallway, up through the only intact stairwell to a roofless classroom with overturned tables and sun-bleached graffiti.

Molly and John move themselves to the least exposed corner of the room after only a minute of disinterested conversation with Matt and me.

You could say I should be surprised. You could say I should feel betrayed, abandoned.

I do.

No matter what spot I move to—sitting on the overturned warped teacher's desk, gazing out a glassless window onto nearby fields ripe with gold-red wheat—Matt follows me. He presses the cool pop can to my arm. I ignore him, move to another spot. When I settle on the edge of the flooring, letting my feet dangle above the wreckage below, Matt squats. He doesn't sit next to me. He *squats*. His stupid gym shorts ride up to bear sunless thighs, thighs that won't know a fond touch for a decade at least. When he prods me with his Mountain Man Screw one last time I take it from him. Stare him dead in the eyes, hold it out from me.

"Why do you think I would want this?"

My smoke comes, and because I have hidden it from them until this point, I turn my head and let it coil into the air, away from him. I take a deep breath, let the demon inside me cool.

"You know where my Dad is?" I ask him. I know that he does. I heard Mrs. Rohr quietly reminding him not to bring it up earlier.

Matt stills. He sits his ass down like a proper human being.

"So you know, and yet you harass me with *this* all day long," I say, squeezing the can. He opens his mouth to respond, but I cut him off. I want to slice his tongue with my interruption. I see what I want. I have to act on it. "You know why you've been bothering me with this shit all day? Because I do. Do you?"

Molly is coming over to us, adjusting her bra strap, John following slow behind.

"You think it's funny?" I ask. "You're going to end up just like him. A waste of breath."

I throw the pop can and its neon-green tin reflects the moon. Milky liquid spreads in an arc before itself, wetting the litter-strewn floor below. I don't hear it hit the ground. The gush of blood in my ears is too strong to hear anything else.

When I finally look away from the ground, I'm alone.

John, Molly, and Matt are at the entrance to the school when I find them. We walk back to the Rohr home in silence.

TWO days later Chung, my mother, and I visit our father at rehab. He's hit the halfway mark in the program and is set to be released on time.

Valley Hope of Atchison contains several modest brick homes, a sprawling cream-painted building with a shaded patio in back. Trimmed lawns. Manicured bushes. Behind the complex, an unruly span of woods.

Our mother was insistent that we all go, and that we all keep secret what we know would devastate him, what would make his six-weeks' progress useless. We don't tell him we've vacated the farm. She doesn't tell him she's separating from him. I can see in her lips, in the twist of her mouth, that she wants to tell him.

For the second time in two weeks, I am hugged. My father clutches to my rib cage. After a moment he picks me up and twirls me around. His tears wet my cheek.

"Chung," our father says, hoisting him up. "Look at this," and he makes Chung flex his arm. "Strong man."

When he sets Chung down, he asks (more to our mother than Chung) how baseball is going. This is the first summer he hasn't coached Chung's baseball team. Chung just squints up at our mother, uncertain how to answer. She doesn't look at our father.

"No sports this summer," she says.

Our father has begun to gain weight, healthy padding around his ribs, his cheeks. For months before he went to rehab he had been thinning out. His frame, his hair, his skin. The catalyst, the thing that had forced our mother to call our grandparents, was the four-inch chemical burn that had ruptured our father's skin, leading from his elbow toward his thumb.

Our mother was convinced he was making meth in some hidden-away space on the farm, and likely smoking most of it, too.

That rehab didn't come earlier was more a symptom of family pride than anything else. Our grandparents refused to face it until the burn ripped his skin open. Until the town dentist said his gums were rotting, until our mother suggested he might blow up the whole farm.

Our mother, father, Chung, and I have lunch together on the rehab center's patio. We have come late, arrived just past two, so our lunch is private. He asks us about summer vacation. Have we done anything fun? We don't know how to answer. He asks us if we've found any new kittens on the farm. We say we haven't. When our mother goes to the restroom, he asks us, "Are you happy to see me? Have you missed me?"

We don't know how to answer.

The afternoon finishes without incident, but as we are leaving, our father pulls me aside, a fresh panic on his face.

"Will you call me next week?"

Chung and our mother don't notice this. They're headed for the van.

"Please. Will you call me? I, I just—," and he can't finish. I can see tears edging their way to the corner of his eyes. "It's so quiet here."

When he lets go of my arm, I say I will. I'll call him. "How about Thursday?

"Thursday's great. Anytime."

WHEN my mother, Chung, and I return to the apartment that evening—it's a three-hour drive back to Salina—we find two notes on our door. One from Kent, written in elegant handwriting on notebook paper. He says he has a couch for us. A friend is moving and doesn't need it anymore. And would we all like to get dinner at Gutierrez's this weekend?

The other note, from our landlord: our rent is late. We need to call him as soon as possible or pay our rent and the late fee.

Our mother balls the second notice and places the first on our fridge.

Dinner with Kent is long. Uncomfortable. It becomes clear that our mother's idea of this affair and Kent's are very different. As our mother refers to this fresh, new start to her life, Kent talks about skyrocketing rent in Salina. About jobs our mother might be interested in. He orders dessert for all of us at the end of the meal, fried ice cream for Chung and me, double chocolate cake for himself and our mother. When our mother suggests sharing one between the two of them, he laughs.

Our mother doesn't laugh. She gets the joke, finally. She's the punchline. He the simple altruist. Her the self-interested fool.

For days after the dinner, she's more brittle than usual. She screams at Chung for not eating his mac 'n' cheese, to which Chung silently retreats to his loft. There's nowhere to escape her in this apartment, unlike the half-dozen sheds and square mile of overgrown fields around the farm. And the endless-seeming sea of prairie beyond. We have little choice but to give in to her. To keep our curses to ourselves.

THE next time I'm dropped off at the Rohr's house, Matt is nowhere to be seen. Molly hardly says a word to me before or during dinner, which Mrs. Rohr passes off as her teenager turned sulky and disobedient. I don't want to correct her.

After dinner I ask Molly what we should do tonight. See what John is doing or go on a walk?

"I don't care. Do whatever you want." She doesn't look up from her dirt-crusted toenails.

I don't know what to say for a while. I lie on her bedroom floor, sweating, staring out the window.

"What I want is to apologize," I make myself say. "I was mean to your brother."

"I don't care about that," she responds, finally making eye contact. "He's a shithead." She goes back to painting her nails. When she brushes a knuckle into a wet nail, she curses and rubs at the mistake with remover so potent my eyes water. "But you should be less mean to boys who like you. Otherwise, you'll always be alone."

I don't respond.

When she finally finishes both feet, she looks to me again. "What bothers me is, who talks about their dad that way? It's—," and she blows on her toes. "It's heartless."

I don't say anything.

We spend the rest of the night like this. Divorced from each other, from the expectation of friendship. I've shown her a part of myself she dislikes, and she's shown a part of herself I envy. Ignorance. Innocence.

ON the day my father and I agreed upon, I tell my mother I am going on a walk and steal her flip phone from her purse on my way out. A levee stretches miles-long by the Smoky Hill River—the closest escape to something not made by human hands in town—a shuddering line of trees framing the river. Three-acre crops of wheat, alfalfa, lay stunted between the man-made earthwork and the river. Crops that have little chance to survive because the land has been deprived its right.

Atop the barricade, I dial him, but the wind proves too fierce to talk on the phone. Further on, near a youth baseball park, the shouts and occasional TINK of balls against metal bats cut through the wind. I stray toward a ten-foot opening in the trees that extends down to the Smokey Hill's riverbank. Heavy rains have made the iron-red water coil and churn, violent against the stormwater's clouds of black silt. I keep my distance. I've had enough of near-drowning for a while. I settle down against a tree and I call him back.

As we talk about the people he has made friends with, about the coming school year, about the harvest season he is missing, I dig my fingers into the soft dirt. I watch the glory of the trees bowing toward the river, pious, and the occasional beaver coasting by. I close my eyes. Imagine a small hut. A dainty fire pit that would light up the flowing waters on chilly nights.

"I don't think I can do this anymore," he says

He has to say it twice, because I don't hear it the first time.

"I can't do this anymore. I want to go home. I want to play *Ocarina of Time* with you and play *Goku* and *Gohan* with Chung. I don't want to be here anymore." His voice is frantic, quickening.

I know he is crying, but I don't know what to say. He is waiting, waiting for me to say something, his breaths uneven. I know that I can't do it; I can't be another person to lie to him—all my life, they've lied to him. I only know that as I hear the quiver in his voice, the desperation, I realize the truth I've been denying myself: I believed we all would come back to the farm, or Chung and I would come back to the farm some day. We would return to where we had been before. Before the lake all I wanted was their separation. Now, torn from the land, I see my mistake. How the country has given me every good thing in my life. How it shaped me. How utterly, utterly lonely life is without it.

"We moved out of the farmhouse. We have an apartment in town. I think you should stay," I tell him.

He goes quiet.

In the silence, my instinct is to lie again. I fight it down.

"It will be better if you stay. Complete the program. I'll convince her to let us visit you again—Dad?"

Still, I hear nothing on the other side. Static. Voices in the background, just outside of comprehension. Eventually, I end the call.

OUR mother figures out within an hour of my return that I told him. She doesn't have to ask me. She doesn't have to acknowledge the misplaced phone or my tear-streaked cheeks. She knows.

That afternoon I hide in my bedroom, hold onto the edge of the accordioned room divider with all that I can. Her voice becomes the wind, inscrutable but deafening, until we break the screen and she takes my hands in one of hers and slaps them for the first time I remember. I say what every teenager says. Hateful things. Reasonable and unreasonable things. I try to imagine Chung is not home, but he is here, as always. He is in his loft, hiding, probably whispering hateful things, but to who? To her. Or to me.

BECAUSE Molly never tells her mother that our friendship is dead, they have me over to their house for a third time in a month. A suffocating number for better friends. Again, we pass pre-dinner and after-dinner in near silence. Matt won't make eye contact with me.

When night comes, I try to convince Molly to go to bed early, cut our time together short, but she has other plans. Shortly after eleven, when both her parents are long gone to bed, she slinks out of the house solo, across the street, initiating a tryst.

I've been preparing for a tryst of my own.

I rise from my sleeping bag when she is out of sight. I grab it and stuff it in my backpack with the supplies I filled it with earlier (clothes, water, granola bars, a few utensils, a pocket knife, a travel-size first-aid kit, my father's battery-powered camping lantern) and tip-toe down the stairs. I find Matt sitting at the bottom. Again. Mountain Dew in hand, again. It's like he knows, has rifled through my bag and figured me out.

"You sneaking off, too?" he whispers. He blocks me from passing. Stands so that we are face to face on the stairs.

Only then do I see the off-color streak in his eyes.

"Move," I say.

He laughs, loud.

I listen for movement in Mr. and Mrs. Rohr's bedroom. "Move," I repeat. "I mean it."

"Aren't you wasting your breath on me?"

I try pushing past him, but he shoves his shoulder forward.

"You owe me an apology."

"Do I?" I ask, growing hot. Flammable. I hold my breath. I try not to look at his eyes, which are red and hyper-focused.

"Take me with you," he says.

"No."

"Take me with you."

"No."

"I know what's wrong with you," he says, circling his fat fingers around my forearm.

"What?" I try moving past him, below the arm that braces the wall, around his soft middle. Can't get through.

"Your—," and he wafts his hand in front of his mouth, and wiggles his fingers like flames, sloshing Mountain Man Screw onto the stairs. "—your . . . Problem."

I listen for movement upstairs, footsteps beyond the front door, but we are alone. I don't know how he has found *this* out also—Amy is the only one who knows, other than my mother and Chung. I don't know whether to admit it, give the sorriest loser in this fucking county that power over me. *Power.*

"It isn't a 'problem,'" I reply, wriggling out of his grip. "I could set this whole place on fire if I wanted to." My swollen hands, now the wrist, too. *Good little girls. Fuck. Fucking flyweights.*

"Hold on," he says, a spark of fear in his eyes.

Apologize? He wants me to apologize?

"Hey," Matt says, bracing my shoulders.

I can barely see him in the haze. All this, and I haven't even needed a fire. My chemistry has been altered. Why shouldn't I alter myself, too?

"Move," I say, watching my smoke curl towards the smoke detector. I have only seconds to get out; get as far as I can before the ringing comes.

Matt disappears in the cloud, goes silent.

I think, *finally, he might let me through.*

And then his hand pulls me upward. He tries his best to drag me back up the stairs. To Molly's room, to his room, or his parents' room, I don't know.

I yank my arm, but he is two years older, stronger.

He is just to the top of the stairs when I finally overpower him. A swift shoulder in the stomach, a whip of my arm. And then we both come crashing down. Mountain Man Screw everywhere. On my face and in my hair. My hip burns and my leg is pins-and-needles, but I manage to stand, grab my backpack, and hobble to the door.

I look back. I see Matt, still on the wood flooring.

And then the ringing comes. I jog down Main Street. Ignore the pain shooting up my leg and back.

OUTSIDE town I find the country in its midnight communion. Whirring locusts, hooting owls, grass folding under gusts of wind, crunching under the paws of soft-footed coyotes. I cry. I don't know exactly where I'm headed. Forgot to plan that part. I walk for an hour or more, through fields, over fences, the moon providing just enough guidance to see shapes on the edge of the world: tree lines, low-rolling hills, a house, distant, brush-shrouded and abandoned.

Before I come upon the place, indistinguishable, half-a-mile from any road, I know this will be it. The earth provides little resistance as I approach. The wind lessens. The world shows itself to me like it hasn't in weeks.

The house is from homesteader times, constructed of limestone, windows shorn of glass, the door rotted away. Only now do I switch on my lantern, now that I am safe inside. Abandoned possessions: an old shoe; dusty glass jars, emerald and ruby; a half-full bag of what was once potatoes; and other ancient stuff scattered among the small rooms. A bed frame caving into the ground. I don't sleep.

When dawn is nearly here, I step outside the front door. The pocket knife, our father's once—I grab it from my backpack and slit a thin line into my palm. Not too deep.

As the sun flays the horizon, I press it to the dirt in the gaping threshold. I say a prayer. I make a promise.

When the time is right, I will bring Chung.
We will live out our days here,
safe from the rabid grasp of others.

I sanitize the cut and wrap my hand in soft cotton.

I look into the coming day. Two beams of light cut past the sun. Cast the world black in their wake.

Freeze

The Brother

FREEZE

CHUNG decided to get lost, and not because his mother had told him to, though she had, and not because his sister had given him that look. *Leave while you can.*

He took Roach Street north. Turned east on Republic. No one but he walked these sidewalks. Cars slowed as they passed, concerned for him. Maybe. Maybe they figured he was crazy, going out in temperatures like this.

Winter Weather Advisory, the TV had shushed under his sister's howl. Snow showers expected, windchills nearing zero. But the apartment had become its own furnace, spouting soot and burning his eyes and nose. His sister's breath became thick with smoke when she got angry or anxious or tired or felt any major emotion other than joy, which was rare. She liked to pretend she had it under control, that her emissions were intentional, but he knew better.

Republic Avenue met Ohio Street and Chung knew unmarked territory awaited him. He walked often but had never passed Ohio before. Here lay the houses of respectable people. No apartments. No dumpsters overflowing with his and his neighbors' lives, open to the public eye. Here lay privacy, where his mother and sister's screams were for their ears only. No concerned or irritated or fed-up neighbors knocking on your door.

Ice blanketed the sidewalks and so he took to the street. A stray cat skittered across its surface twenty feet off, ears flat, muscles trembling in flight. "Take cover when the animals take theirs," his mother would warn. "They're wiser than you'll ever be."

Still, Chung didn't turn back. He followed Republic to Faith Drive, spotted a park in the distance, its stunted oaks and sun-grayed play equipment stunning against the unburdening sky. Snow melted into the knitting of his hat, collected on the smooth polyester of his coat. He could stay here a while, really let the freeze cut into him. When he got this cold, he was reminded of the lake where he and his sister almost drowned a few years back. How after such a short time his body felt in sync with the water's rolling, his blood matched in temperature with the water. He hadn't felt a harmony so clean since.

A plastic bag wafted past him, flying higher as it moved away from him. The wind carried it across the short field of the park, over the levee. Chung followed it.

On the levee's graveled top, he spied a stretch of trees a baseball field away. The bag caught in a low-hanging branch, and when Chung approached, its metered snap rasped in Morse code, or so Chung thought. *D-O-O-R*. Like his sister and his mother and her mother before her, he knew that some beacons must be recognized. That couriers of better truths came in unexpected forms.

Snow dusted the treeline and in its serpentine crawl, Chung discovered a river lazing behind it. He crossed the crunching grass, found a trail down to the bank, muddied from overuse. Across the landing lay discarded packs of cigarettes, frosted beer cans, and the slick, gaudy wrappers of condoms, whose use he'd begun to contemplate more and more. He cleared himself a spot, felt the chill of the earth against his legs as he sat down. Ice had frozen over the surface of the river, leaving only the edges free and coiling amidst the disruption.

The lake. The sinking. How time slowed when he and his sister were under. His sister's smoke had come soon after, and he—he had come up altered, too. The smallest trouble floored him, stripped his vision, and contorted him. Where his sister had gained in strength, he floundered. Often, he wondered if deep inside him some yet unseen power waited— would make him more than his current useless self. If not smoke, why not an ability to breathe underwater? Why not a core of ice to tame his sister's fire? But no. If anything, he had been hollowed out by the near-drowning, a void that grew over time, that had to be crammed full or otherwise capped if he was to be of any use to anyone.

Though he had ventured out in all the wintry clothing he owned, his toes numbed in his boots and his fingers stuck together. His breath came as white spears, falling on the hard-packed ground. A fox watched him from across the river. A whistling wound through the trees and reminded him of his mother and sister.

Not so long ago, when Chung was alone in the apartment, his mother at her small auto-dealership job, and his sister roaming the country with her new friends, Amy and June, he had flipped through his sister's magazines, secret, coveted each impressionable page. Didn't mind the grease of his fingers leaving their marks. Didn't care for the makeup tutorials or the *Which Season Are You?* quizzes. He ran his thumb over the shirtless, beachy photos of Matthew McConaugheys and Nick Carters. He pictured the carving of their cheekbones, their sweat-shorn foreheads cast under the golden light of his tiny bedroom. But then the rounded eye of a front-facing Channing Tatum broke him out of his reverie, his gaze too direct. Living. And so Chung flipped five, ten pages down, until he found a story framed by illustrations of ice-melt-skinned blond-haired men and women and children in swimsuits against a snow-washed sky. They leapt, suspended mid-air, a black pool of water reeling below their feet. *Polar Plunge Keeps You Healthy and Young,* a garish title claimed. Apparently, Norwegians and Scandinavians practiced polar plunges—jumping into icy waters following exercise or the sauna—for centuries in order to rejuvenate their muscles, promote circulation, and, potentially, improve their immune systems. The language of the article proved hyperbolic, and its quotes mostly came from Northeasterners who claimed *a better connection to their European roots* after participating in the plunges. On the last page of the article, a photo splayed Russian citizens, cast in stark blacks and whites, facing down a cross carved out of a frozen lake. Apparently, Russians too, partook in plunges, though they did it, reportedly, for Jesus—to celebrate the Epiphany. To honor the cathartic power of water.

The ice-carved cross came to Chung's mind now, peering down the rigid face of the river. Yes. He needed a reset. An awakening of his own cast his blood to boil, his heart to shivering. Chung stepped forward, toes inches from the water.

As if responding to his movement, suddenly, the water ceased its churning. Thickened to ice.

Wonder, Heat, frustration, rose to Chung's cheeks. He bent down, picked up a rock, raised it up, up high and threw it down with all his twelve-year-old might.

The rock bounced, skidded five, ten feet downstream.

Chung's breaths caught in his throat, usually a signal that his blackouts, his flailings, were minutes, seconds away. He held his breath, knelt to remove his shoes and socks. He stripped his pants and coat and shirts and knit hat. So agitated was his body that the cold kept its distance.

He stepped, gingerly at first, for he didn't really believe in the river's rebellion. He ventured to the river's center, toes neither losing color nor melting the partition denying him entry. When the ice grew utterly unrelenting, thick as limestone, Chung jumped, kicked his knees to his chest, stuck out his fists, arms to wings, and pounded his bare feet and all the weight of his slim body into the ice.

Nothing.

He raised his leg, as he had done in Tae Kwon Do all those years ago, and beat the ice with the heel of his foot.

Nothing.

He was stomping, thrashing, wild, when he noticed the snow-misted fox approach from the side. He paused, felt, finally, the thundering in his chest and head, the lift of his oxygen-loaded brain. He watched the fox, its little claws kissing the ice, its back arching playfully before, with too knowing a gaze, it sank to its back, stomach to sky, languid tongue to cheek.

Chung thought to pet it or pick it up or mirror its prone posture, an offering, but before he could, his muscles strained, throat closed, vision clouded, and all that white fell to black.

II.

DRIFT

Communion at a Taco Bell

The Sister

COMMUNION AT A TACO BELL IN GYPSUM, KANSAS

AMY decides on our tread over gravel-pocked pavement that Taco Bell has come to Gypsum. To the empty lot at the far edge of town. I don't have the heart to tell her she's wrong, that Taco Bell isn't coming, never will, to this hundred-acre town. That these century-old shacks and cracked-open ruins, the ghost of a gas station that never was, the singular breath of the only church, the only convenience store, the only paved road, are nothing to Yum Brands and its twenty-billion-dollar empire. I don't have the heart to tell her we're sooner to spy the golden arches spearing this million-acre sky than to smell the synthetic, libidinous aroma of nacho cheese pervade every block; to tell her that we too have no stakes in this town. We are farm girls and thus homeless among the prairies.

We come here when our fathers are drunk and our mothers are whistle-voiced kettles, spouting steam. We come here all through junior high and high school. Sometimes I sneak the car keys and drive from Salina. Sometimes I'm dropped off. No matter what, Amy insists I pedal her bike from the Badillo's farm to Gypsum while she stands on the back axle's hollow metal pegs , body weight pressed into her palms pressed into my back, fingernails marking their half-moons along my collarbones until, in the half-moon light, we see it—

GYSPUM
NEXT
13 EXITS

—as if every street is an off-ramp, every sodium-orange streetlamp a beacon for a parallel world (where Taco Bells are built in hundred-acre towns).

Tonight. July's boiling wind. Blanched wheat fields line our path, left over from the farmer who scattered his brain across his fourth-generation farmhouse. Coyotes, two or twenty miles away, fill our ears with laughter, with communion. A poor flattened possum denied burial catches our eye, strewn along the shallow shoulder, and we promise to cradle his body into the earth on our return, hands like shovels, bent knees like prayer. Two sixteen-year-old deviant farm girls.

Amy, my first and only real friend, was the first to show me that rubbing raw earth into the eyes of haters could be more than just revenge, spitting between teeth, more than just the poison we uttered; that showing you had worth was more than just, but our land-given right. Amy, who first showed me the glamor of crudity in her sun-bled cheeks, met everyone but me with a *"fuck you, Johnny"* or *"kiss the earth and beg forgiveness, sinner,"* as if every other warm body was our own personal nemesis. Our world perfected, whittled down to us-and-them, made our time apart (which was most of the time) that much lonelier.

Amy taught me in her selfless vulgarity what love could be. I had never loved anyone in any real way before I met her, but of course it took two spirit sisters—born among the same skin-splitting, head-crushing prairie machinery, with the same legacies of iron-wrought pain and fertilized death—to find the meaning of love. The meaning of love is:

WELCOME TO GYPSUM
GOOD CHURCHES
GOOD SCHOOLS
GOOD PEOPLE

—minus the schools. No schools anymore (except the hard-knocks, chest-breached, glass-veined, meth-lab kind) and a questionable number of good people and only one Methodist church (which was once a Catholic church, which was once another open field, most sacred of all).

The hot asphalt below our feet speaks, breath acrid as sulfur and steaming. All things are possible, it says. If our callused soles can touch its scarred skin, so too can this town bear the purpled glow of that monolith, filling the palest gray parking lot with trauma-shorn customers (because Gypsum is nothing if not marked by strife). Imagine that light piercing every window, reflecting against every chipped-white home until all you see shimmers.

What the road fails to tell us is that along with this promised gift so too can two promising farm girls live to see that purpled glow flicker off. A snapped finger, a shelled dream (because Gypsum is nothing if not marked by loss).

"What is the first thing you'll order?" Amy asks me.

"I've heard the Crunchwrap Supreme is good," I say. I see the glow now, at the end of the road, summoned by our hungry hearts.

"You've *heard* it's good?" She braces my shoulders where the ghosts of her fingernails still dig deep. "You've had Taco Bell before, right?"

I keep my eyes on the purple light, which is even richer than I had expected, closer to us than we could have wished for.

"Well—" I begin, because my mother never allowed us to eat "such tasteless shit" in the past, and even after our mother left our father during his rehabilitation and moved us to Salina, *a city,* and even after I have a car, I haven't been able to bring myself to drive into Salina's gray-cold concrete lot alone, without Amy, to taste its nacho cheese. Because the truth is, I know nothing of Taco Bell, and never will, except that Amy values it, understands the impact it might have on Gypsum, our small, hollowed-out town, because it is, in some ways, always *our* town, *our* abandoned lot. And the truth is that I need her, and I still need to believe that Taco Bell is coming to Gypsum, that our streetlamps are beacons that glow like harbor lights at the end of this great grassy sea.

"—It doesn't matter," Amy says. "You're going to try every goddamn menu item when it gets here."

Her hands release my shoulders and I feel that sway, of the earth turned aqueous, the air burning with salt.

The glow is flickering now, but I tell myself it is only to encourage us, to lead us closer to shore. As I take her hand and march toward it, I hold my breath. I pray against what I know must come.

A snapped finger. A shelled dream. A failed communion.

Kindling

The Sister

KINDLING

"DON'T get one of them killed," Jordan's mother said on the drive to Rock Springs, a campground just south of Junction City. "You've never been good at keeping things alive."

Jordan rolled down the window to strip her mother's smoke from the car.

"You're worried I'll get one of them killed, instead of worrying I'll turn them," Jordan said. She looked forward to shaping her little campers, eight little girls, with her wisdom, forming them into proper, dour, bitter young women like herself.

When her mother dropped her off, she flicked her live cigarette into the gravel and said that no matter what happened, she wouldn't be picking her up until the camp ended. This was *her* vacation, *her* break from the chaos of their kinship, too.

Amy and June waited for Jordan at the mess hall, Amy flicking her own cigarette into the dry brush spreading out from the building.

"What do you want to bet this is just a front," Amy said.

"Meth?" June asked.

"Sex trafficking," Amy whispered. "We're about to get fucked."

Already, Jordan felt the little thrill of their words, like they were playing out a movie she had watched dozens of times.

The girls stepped inside the mess hall. They found six slack-jawed boys and three other girls, their co-counselors. A bullish man, the director, and his limp-haired assistant stood on a small stage next to a blue-lit projector screen. All watched as Amy—who was the kind of girl to illicit wide-eyed stares—strolled to the front row and collapsed into a chair, legs spread out in front of her, maximizing her territory. Jordan noted that the director was among the rubbernecked, though she couldn't tell if it was out of lechery or horror that he stared, because Amy had held onto a puff of cigarette smoke until the moment she flopped down.

When the director snapped to, he coughed and pulled up a PowerPoint on the screen. He began the training session by telling all of them how important they were. How they were about to mold young minds for the better. Jordan took notes at first, but abandoned the act when she realized the camp director and his assistant had little guidance to offer. The dusty rafters echoed the clichés back at them, so their effect was doubly lessened. *Be kind. Lead by example. Find common ground and build from there.*

"You are likely the only person standing between these kids and a meth problem in ten years." Trade that with alcohol or tobacco or cocaine and you had the whole lesson.

The director and his assistant went over the rules for campers:

- NO BOYS IN GIRLS' CABINS AND NO GIRLS IN BOYS' CABINS
- NO TOBACCO, ALCOHOL, OR OTHER DRUGS ALLOWED (OBVIOUSLY)
- NO FIREARMS ON CAMPUS (which pissed off the kid from Herrington)
- NO SEXUAL ACTIVITY OF ANY KIND

Toward the end of the training, everyone gathered in a circle for a refresher on CPR, which hadn't been required for counselors but was strongly encouraged.

Amy was the first to volunteer. This Jordan had anticipated. Her friend was always eager to perform: cheerleading, debate, and choir filled up her afternoons. Jordan's were filled with the drone of the same *Law & Order* episodes revolving on her mother's television and the booming gunshots of her little brother's video games. Add to this the stench of smoke, cooking something inside her. A summer of agony, a blackening world.

Jordan hated summer because it meant more time at home. Camp had been her only solace as a kid, and as a teenager a welcome job.

Amy bent over the glistening blank-eyed dummy. She arched her back and scanned the room for a proper male counselor to direct her mouth-to-mouth at, until her eyes landed on a boy with enormous cheeks and tiny ears who showed no sign of coercion. Hers was an obscene show, and at the end, the director clapped and declared, "Very good," before asking if anyone wasn't in fact certified.

June was the first to speak up, but instead of offering herself as volunteer, she mimicked Jordan's voice, low and monotone. "I'm not certified." It was a lie, a vile lie that Jordan would make June pay for later. She pushed Jordan into the middle of the circle.

Before Jordan could explain or smear the puce-and-gray linoleum with her friend's blood, the director was pressing on her shoulder, asking her to kneel.

"I don't want to," she said. The dummy's lack of gaze, lack of any human character, unsettled her.

It could have been the implication of following Amy's porno audition or the director (too large and too loud a breather) standing behind her, but Jordan froze. She stared into the dummy's non eyes. Its gray-green pallor made acid gargle up her throat.

"First," the director said, "first you do compressions."

Jordan pounded its chest and leaned down to push air into its non-lungs, but the stench of the plastic made her gag. When she came up to do compressions again, her palms, sweating, slipped off the non-sternum and sent the prop flying toward someone's knees and her hands toward the floor, where her wrist twisted against the tile.

"That's alright," the director said. "Chet's used to getting tossed around." He threw the dummy toward Amy who tossed it to June who sent it sailing into the arms of a dead-white kid from Hays.

It became a running joke after that, *Jordan and Chet sitting in a tree,* and if anyone forgot about the incident, her inflamed, useless wrist would bring it all back to them.

THE kids arrived in buses from six different schools across central Kansas. Each counselor would have seven or eight kids, all between fifth and sixth grades, all surely as insincere in their anti-drug resistance as their teenage counselors. Jordan was stuck with two kids from Hays, one from Junction City, three from Salina, and two from her own school, which was small enough that she already knew the two girls by name though she'd never talked to them before. One girl was serpentine and green-eyed, Taryn, the other mulish and blue-eyed with a wild mane of ratty black hair, Rory.

The two from her school were good girls. That much she could rely on. They warmed a place in her deeply rural heart. But the others? They became browbeat in the first hour of camp by a white-haired Dutch girl. While Jordan was out, they wrote insults along the wall behind her bunkbed. She was filing paperwork on Rory's medical needs (asthma, bee allergy, eczema, and IBS—why she was sent off to camp in the middle of the country, Jordan didn't know), which didn't take more than ten minutes. She came back to the entirety of the wall scratched over.

Jordan isn't a girl's name. Jordan smells like manure. Jordan can suck a big fat one. Jordan should change her name to Biddy because she's so old.

To be fair, they weren't the only phrases scratched into the walls. Decades worth of scribblings bitched about evil counselors or the depthless lake or the bullish camp director and his assistant.

Jordan wondered how many more decades those walls could sustain. She'd heard the director mooing to his assistant about the recent drop in attendance. No one believed in these anti-drug campaigns anymore. They'd even cut the marijuana segment since Jordan had gone as a camper six years before; no one bought it, that weed was fatal, or that it was Satanists' favorite pastime anymore. Well, many Kansans *did* still believe those things, but the state had entertained legalizing it recently.

All the counselors knew the camp programming didn't work. Both Jordan's parents had attended this camp almost forty years ago and look where that landed them.

Jordan herded the girls to swimming and lanyard-making and the DUI-driving lesson where they all wore goggles that fractured the world into a hundred misplaced shards. Most girls couldn't clear more than a few yards behind the wheel of a much-less-lethal golf cart, let alone a car. That night, before lights out, Jordan, Amy, and June met in Amy's cabin, where the girls were all already in bed—Amy the perfect drill sergeant. The three friends each strapped on a pair of DUI goggles and tried to snatch the others' off first, until they all ended up pressed against the walls, too woozy to stand free.

When lights out came, the counselors went back to their respective cabins. It took half an hour for Jordan to demand and shout and beg her girls to get in their beds, to turn off their goddamn phones. *Who has phones when you're twelve?* She asked nobody, though the truth was that most kids did by then.

Jordan lay in her top bunk, half-asleep, when she heard movement. She stayed still at first, cautious of her little demons' likely attacks.

"Jordan," a voice whispered, "Jordan. You aren't really asleep are you?"

She opened her eyes to see Amy's over-plucked eyebrows rippling above the side of her mattress. Amy hopped onto the empty bunk below. She dug her elbows into Jordan's ribs, and propped her head on her hands, fingernails freshly painted. The reek of the polish burned Jordan's nose.

"Good," Amy said. "The first rule of flirtation is to bring your gawky friend, so that boys remember what options are out there."

Jordan punched Amy's elbows away, so that her chin smacked against the plastic liner of the mattress. Jordan had a roiling love for Amy and Amy an obsession akin to affection so that this was their love language: punched arms and nail-stabbed stomachs.

"I'm kidding," Amy said, stepping down from the bunk below. Jordan sat up and slid down the side of her bunk. June arose from the black, leaning on Amy's shoulder.

"We also know Jordan would rather drop arsenic in a boy's pop than kiss him," June added, "So, yes, good choice."

"Not true," Jordan repeated. "Arsenic is too clean."

THE girls found them comparing foot lengths by the pool. There was the gun-fanatic Herrington boy, squat and goat-faced and ready to charge. There was a timid-looking ginger, the big-cheeked boy from Hays, and then there was a new face Jordan hadn't noticed before. He had the upper body of a swimmer and lower body of a wrestler, long and then short. Sinewy and then bulging. His hair was iridescent, his face not unlike a fox. He was beautiful. He was the most gorgeous, immaculate figure Jordan had ever seen. Already, she was forming prayers about his green eyes homing in on her.

The girls weighed their options, given there were four boys and three girls. Amy sidled next to Big Cheeks, claws retracted—and June, the ginger. Jordan approached the athletic chimera hesitantly, every movement steeped in cost, in possible rejection. They all perched on the pool ledge, boy-girl-boy-girl-boy-girl-boy, dangling their feet into the water. Five minutes of stunted banter passed between them:

TO AMY: You don't look like a girl from Salina.

FROM AMY: I'm not. I'm from that raw, blood-curdling nightmare you wake up screaming to. I'm from that dark corner of your bedroom. I'm from somewhere you've never seen and will *definitely* never know.

FROM JUNE: Prove you have a soul, sinner. Prove your fealty to the Great Glorious God on High, or I swear to Him, little Ginger Boy, I swear, I, yes, me, will smite you in the name of our Lord. Prove it, Pretty Boy, if you want to live.

TO JUNE: *silence, and then a loud, gurgling kiss that lasted longer than Jordan stuck around.*

TO JORDAN (FROM THE CHIMERA): Jordan, is it? I like that name. So you're a farm girl. You don't smell like manure.

FROM THE GUN-FANATIC GOAT: She smells like, like asphalt, right? And she smells like honey.

FROM THE CHIMERA (SNIFFING THE AIR): honey! That's it. Sugar and acid.

FROM JORDAN (TO THE BOTH OF THEM): And you both reek of Axe. Seriously, what seventeen-year-old still wears Axe?

"Do you think guys buy this shit? Our aunts won't stop sending us value packs," the goat said, brushing off Jordan's insult.

"Yeah, no kidding. I got four cans of it last Christmas," the chimera added.

Jordan hated his beauty. She wanted to snuff it out of him.

"I swear, I only spray it around my pits," the chimera waved his hands over his body. "My lower half is untouched."

"Same," the goat added.

The chimera sniffed the air again. "Is something burning?"

"Jordan, cool it," Amy called from the end of the line. She apparently had found Big Cheeks less desirous than before and slid into the pool in her gym shorts and camisole. She swam toward Jordan and her limbs wriggled and ballooned under the water. Jordan tried to look away. She rose and ignored her friend and the two boys trying to convince her to stay. Threatening to throw her in the pool.

She was halfway to the pool house when they (the chimera and the goat) trotted up from behind.

"We were just kidding," the chimera said.

"You don't have to leave," the goat added.

"I'm tired," she replied, still yearning for a reason to stay.

A hope rose up as the chimera turned his head to one side, rushed into a closet cut into the pool house.

"If you don't like us," the chimera called from the black little space, "maybe you'll like him." The chimera resurfaced with Chet, the nauseating dummy, hugged against his chest, so that Chet's non-eyes were level with Jordan's.

"Yeah," the goat bleated. "Give him some sugar, why don't you?"

Jordan, of course, punched the dummy out of the chimera's arms with her good fist, and pushing past them, of course, cursed their names "to fucking hell and back again."

Amy called after her but didn't leave the pool to follow her.

This, Jordan wouldn't forgive.

THE chimera led Cabin B. The goat, Cabin D. This she knew from the training sessions the day before. Jordan knew she should wait until morning, when their cabins were empty, but she was impatient. B was quiet enough, all the tweenish boys perfectly asleep. It was easy enough to find the chimera's duffel bag, which was stuffed under the only empty bunk bed. She lifted its hole-riddled straps just enough so that the bag didn't scrape against the floor as she pulled it out. She planted one hand along the closed zipper and her index finger and thumb around the zipper clip, opening it tooth by tooth. Far too pissed to be squeamish, she dug out the chimera's briefs. She found only one pair, even though they would be at camp all week.

Jordan was careful to spray directly down and to turn her face away. The pepper spray, even used in such small doses, scattered into the air and set her skin aflame. When the fabric was properly doused, she slid the briefs back into the bag, zipped it shut, and ran out of the cabin, clawing for fresh air.

The mace had been a gift from her mother for her seventeenth birthday. *Don't get yourself murdered,* she would say. *If you insist on walking at night,* which Jordan always did, trekking the long gravel-laid levee to the river, her only escape from the slow rot of the town, *you need to be prepared for night folk.* There hadn't been a murder in her hometown in five years, and that had been a domestic issue.

The spray, Jordan had read, was nearly as strong as bear mace, and half as strong as the police-grade stuff that closed up people's airways and left them blind and weak for hours after. Jordan had once seen a video of some unnamed protest where officers had sprayed people who were sitting, arms interlocked. After, other people came and poured milk over the protester's faces and arms, but still they cried out in pain and confusion, the world, she imagined, wrought down to its core aching darkness.

Cabin D proved similarly quiet. The goat's bunk bed was all the way at the back of the room. The scant moonlight and flicker of a distant lamp through a window showed her this much. She knelt by the empty bed, pried open the cavity of the goat's backpack, apparently the only bag he had brought for the trip. She felt the ring below plastic that was an unused condom. She fingered through torn t-shirts and crusty tennis shoes, until she felt the elastic band of a pair of boxers. Digging deeper, she found a second pair.

She was mid-spray on the second pair when another sound rose up from inside the cabin. Like a cat licking its fur. Repetitive and wet. Jordan peered around the dark room as she sprayed the goat's boxers in mace. It was a boy masturbating, she realized, under the covers, thank God.

She gagged. She needed to puke. From the mace, from the sound.

In Jordan's distraction, her mace-dowsing hand slacked. The naked tops of her feet ran slick with pepper spray. She cursed and kicked the backpack under the bed and did a belly-crawl back through the cabin, praying the boy wouldn't hear her, that no one would bear witness to her transgression. She'd already broken a core rule twice: no girls in boys' cabins.

When she made it to the door, stomach and thighs covered in floor shit, she kissed the sweet earth.

She did her puking in the woods behind the cabins. She crept back into her own cabin and into her bed. She was too afraid to wash her feet, to make her demon girls aware of the bad, righteous thing she had done. She didn't sleep from the pain of the spray flaring across her skin. As the hours passed and the sun rolled into view, she cried a little for the sleep she had lost, and for the glory to come, two jackasses reeling in pain.

Jordan was disappointed to learn, at breakfast, that the chimera, that star child, had not in fact begun his morning running and screaming from a burning bush. Apparently, he hadn't changed underwear from night to morning.

She blessed the earth for showing her the chimera was not the god his looks promised. He was just like any other shit-stain she had met before. The goat, too, proffered no stories of agony. It appeared he, too, hadn't slipped on a fresh pair of underwear before leading his cabin out to the lake.

Jordan didn't swim. She let Amy and June lead her own campers in the pathetic, girls-only session in synchronized swimming. *Kick your legs like this, girls, to do the eggbeater. Kick your legs like you live off the water, like you've never stepped foot on dry land before. No, idiot. Like this. Loosen your feet, for fuck's sake.*

As her friends led the children in the planned choreography, the chimera and the goat approached her on the beach.

"Not a swimmer?" the goat asked.

"Nope."

"Well, we want to say we're sorry," the chimera said. The goat nodded and moaned a sorrowful echo.

"We were dicks to you. We actually think you're pretty cool."

Jordan ignored them. *Tricksters, petty fools.*

"We were wondering," the chimera said, waning repentant, hands folded and eyes lowered, "if you would come with us tonight."

"Where?" Jordan asked, flicking a stray shard of glass toward their feet.

"The cave."

"I'm not going into a cave with anybody."

"Your friends are going, too," the goat said. "We have a whole group. I'd be devastated if you didn't come."

"And you?" Jordan directed at the chimera. That disappointment of a beast.

"I'd rather choke dead on vomit than not see you there."

"Fine," she said, getting up and pacing over to the water. She got just deep enough that her ankles were submerged.

"Jordan! Join us! Join us!" cried the girl from her school, Rory, so doomed and yet so keen on being good and happy and all-sweet.

Jordan raised up her arms and did a kick-dance, mimicking the girls' swimming, raising up her own little disturbance in the water. The girl cheered and hooted and reached for the sky in joy, cast iridescent against the watery spray.

BEFORE the end of the day's activities, the camp director and his assistant called all the counselors into the mess hall. "Just checking how things are going," they said.

Jordan didn't believe that. They knew. She knew they knew. She had crept into not one, but two boys' cabins. The masturbator had told them, or another sly kid had seen her and waited until mid-day to report her.

"First," the assistant said, leaning his sopping palms against an indoor picnic table, "We want to reiterate. No tobacco please." He looked to the Herrington gun-boy. "No chew," and to Amy, "no cigarettes. Please. It sends a confusing message to the kids."

"Second," the camp director said, hovering above them, "please behave yourselves, *even after* all the campers are in bed."

Jordan's throat stirred with fire. She knew it. She knew that furry-handed little fucker had ratted on her.

"No more poolside chats."

Before Jordan could process her relief, Amy's arm shot up in the air. By the flick of her wrist and twist of her ribcage, Jordan knew she was on the prowl. But for who? Big Cheeks? Not likely.

"What about misbehaving ourselves when the kiddos are at crafts? How about during lunch?" She shrugged like a marionette pulled by anxious hands. A play at coy naivete that might have worked if her voice was higher than a low alto. "I can't behave *all the time.* No one can! When is the right time to not behave?"

Jordan cringed, and the assistant director crowed, *"Enough! Enough!"*

They all went back to their little ill-behaved, sure-to-be-drug-addict devils. The counselors finished their sessions for the day, tucked their little devils in their little devil beds, and met at the edge of the woods at nine. The cave ended up being nothing more than a small burrow that used to house (Jordan guessed) a family of badgers. It lay just off the south side of the lake, far enough from the cabins and camp director's house that their little fire would go unnoticed.

The chimera brought along Chet the dummy but promised not to taunt Jordan with it.

"Promise."

He bowed, sat down next to her, and Jordan watched the firelight ripple across his back. The goat drifted off into the water and didn't resurface for twenty minutes. June stayed engrossed with her ginger, and the few other girls who had come huddled all to one side, whispering ghost stories to each other, too afraid to let the stories catch the wind and come to life.

Jordan inched so close to the fire that her mace-burned feet prickled from the heat. Blisters began to form at her heels. The chimera gently grasped each of Jordan's feet and slid them back, away from danger.

"Where are you from again?" the magical boy asked.

Jordan wanted to smash his perfect face in-between her palms.

"A farm outside Salina," she said. "But I live mostly in town now, with my mom."

The chimera didn't blink. He leaned in, and for a moment Jordan believed great forces were at work. She closed her eyes and waited for the sloppy hot kiss that was gods-sent to her. Dead fish and algae wafted in from the lake.

"Where are you really from?" the beautiful boy asked, a question Jordan often heard, because even though she looked whiter than her brother, even though she was white, if you boiled things down and asked how the world saw her (how it treated her compared to him), it was her eyes that brought these questions.

You just look different, well-meaning people would say. Or less-well-meaning people would say: *you look exotic, like a doll. You know?*

"Like—your family," the chimera continued. "Where did they come from?" Like she couldn't understand him, needed hand-holding.

"Hell," Jordan responded, smoke choking up her throat. "I'm a spawn of Satan. Can't you see my damned feet?" She pointed at the red-hot swaths of skin. She stood and anchored her image against the flame, so the chimera would really have something to think about in his days-old underwear that night.

 "You shouldn't have messed with the devil's daughter. Don't you know this? Didn't your parents teach you that much?"

Jordan was about to walk off, to curl into her cool bed and think only of that flame casting her in enigmatic light, when the chimera stood, too.

The goat had returned from the waters and was trudging his swampy way up toward them.

"Creature from the deeps," he groaned, sending his eyes in two directions. "Bewareeee."

Before Jordan could tell the goat just how piss-poor-an-excuse-of-a-man he was, before she could slink back to her bed, the goat had his hands on her, the chimera was grabbing her ankles.

They carried her like a swinging hammock.

They waded knee deep in the water, then waist deep, and she thrashed and bit at the goat's neck.

Finally, she grasped a chunk of his hair and pulled and pulled until he released her, and the chimera lost his footing and dropped her legs, and then she was submerged, she was blind and cold and frozen in time, unable to think or breathe or swim like a normal teenager.

She was drowning in four feet of water.

Chet, the CPR dummy, appeared above her, contours lit by the distant campfire, but as Jordan reached for his plastic body, her swollen wrist straining, her fingers slipped, and his torso swept on and on, farther into the lake's black belly.

JORDAN woke to Amy's cherry-glossed lips moving away from hers. Apparently the two boys had frozen when they realized what was happening. They just stood there and watched.

Jordan spit up water and a little more. She shivered and belly-crawled toward the fire.

"Thank God," they all said.

They sat next to her and offered her their sweat-stained shirts and ratty towels, and though she had decided on hating every last one of them, their warmth comforted her.

That night they didn't tell the camp director or his assistant about their fellow co-counselor's baffling near-catastrophe. They didn't break the camp's final rule, no sexual activity, either. Every counselor hunched back into their cabins, sad but relieved (if they were honest) that the night's expectations had been dashed.

On her way, Jordan found Amy standing in the middle of the gravel path, facing the director's cabin. A singular light flickered from inside.

Jordan pushed past her without a second glance, but long into the night stood watching at her cabin's screen window as Amy sucked down cigarette after cigarette until the director's light blinked away and she was left wheezing in the dark.

IN the morning, Jordan commanded her campers with an iron first. She had come back from that void bolder than she had ever been before. She grabbed a girl by the back of her shirt when she wouldn't leave the cabin for their daily no-drugs-or-you'll-die-at-eighteen video sessions. The girls watched her in bowl-eyed interest after that. That night, they were dead quiet, and for once, Jordan thought she might have a chance at bending the devil campers and dull-brained boys to her will.

In the shower the next day, the second-to-last day of camp, Jordan felt weightless, buoyed by the chimera and goat's newfound tenderness toward her, by her friends' careful attention. She set off back to her cabin, feeling the fresh heat of the sun meeting the trees, basking in the glory of her momentary haven. When she passed out of the sun, her world swirled like over-exposed film, all reds and blurriness. She saw two campers, the white-haired Dutch girl and Taryn, the less-fragile girl from her school, run screaming through the screen door.

Jordan prayed their hysteria was produced by a spider or unexpected brown scorpion. The camp had hundreds lurking in the shadows. Inside, she found chaos amid a wet, sticky haze. Immediately her eyes burned, and she rubbed at them with her arm but to no avail. She was halfway to her bunk bed when she saw the pepper-spray canister lying in the middle of the floor.

She spied her duffel bag splayed open and all its contents scattered, and knew that her presumption of power, of control over her demon-girls, had been foolish. They were still as poorly behaved, just secretly.

The girls were in a frenzy of agony and terror because, as Jordan now saw, the asthmatic girl, Rory, was slumped against the wall and audibly wheezing. She was awake, that much was clear. Her chest shuddered; her mouth wet her shirt with drool.

Jordan crawled through the mess of clashing girls, praying that she remembered the girl's bed correctly, that she identified the purple unicorn backpack correctly. She dug inside, fingers cutting against jagged book edges and catching in the rings of a notebook. No, it wasn't this one. Rory's backpack had been pink, had been decorated in horses, not unicorns. Jordan searched, the pain of her swollen wrist and irritated eyes, nose, throat, numbed by the adrenaline pushing her closer to her destination.

She found the inhaler. She dragged the girl out of the cabin as the others huddled around the entrance, crying and rubbing at their raw skin. Jordan led the girl through her inhalations. Breathe in, in, in. Hold, hold, hold. Out, out, out. Repeat.

Jordan led the eight not-devils-but-small-crying-girls to the camp director's house. He would know what to do, would have the right ointments to soothe the girls' skin, the presence of mind to call an ambulance for the asthmatic girl who, despite her measured inhalations, did not improve.

The director's house stood empty.

Jordan searched the cabins and the mess hall. The stables and the lake. Nothing.

She paced in front of the director's cabin. She begged the goat and the chimera and Big Cheeks and the ginger to please help her, to save her darling girl from choking to death, to save herself from the damnation that was to come. Please, please, please, release her. Still they proved useless, and it was only then that she recognized what she had been reluctant to admit all along. That given the choice, she would rather be hated than forgotten. And so, when they had gathered all around her—the chimera and the goat and Big Cheeks—she summoned up a slurry of insults corrosive enough to make Satan himself cry.

Then Jordan spotted a flash of light, infinitesimal, in the woods. She stumbled through the thick brush and rotten logs until she came upon Amy smoking a cigarette before a deep dip in the earth.

Amy nodded toward Jordan when she came into view.

"I need your help," Jordan hadn't calmed. She was heaving, smoking, desperate for this agony to end. "I need to find the camp director."

Amy smiled. She nodded toward the pit. Flicked her ash into its belly.

Jordan peered down to see the director struggling to pull himself up by a root. He was smeared in dirt and beet red.

Jordan later learned that Amy had led the director, who had been undeniable in his attention to her, deeper into the knee-high brush, that he had watched with sun-washed anticipation as she held her lit cigarette inches from the dead grass, casting fire-hot ash downward, ready for the earth to engulf them. That she had found the pit the day before and led him straight into it, an ankle-twisting, head-banging fall. For half an hour, Amy had stood above the director, chain-smoking, and tossing her butts in his direction, ordering him to throw his wallet up before she helped him, scattering his IDs and YMCA and Frequent-Bowler cards across the forest floor, until finally, Jordan showed up.

When the girls helped him out and they emerged from the trees, the director ignored the both of them. Jordan had informed him of the situation, and he sprinted ahead of them.

By the time Amy and Jordan got back to the director's cabin, the camp nurse had already arrived, summoned by the limp-haired assistant who had the presence of mind to call her. The girl, Rory, would be fine, the nurse said. Jordan's other girls were freshly slathered in calming milk. Every failure she had visited on her campers had been rectified by more capable adults.

Before the director's diatribe could come, Jordan drifted away from the camp. She waded out into the lake. Got waist deep. She missed the cool breath of the water, the give of the swallowed earth. She contemplated sinking, giving her ribs, shoulders, neck, and all to the lake, but instead she stayed perfectly still and forgot for a moment what it was to be one thing, forever failing on her own, and lived, just for the moment, as if all the world was hers to claim.

Six Days of Peace

The Brother

SIX DAYS OF PEACE

AFTER weeks of anticipation, Chung's mother dropped his sister off at Rock Springs campgrounds outside Junction City. His sister, Jordan, would spend six days counseling eleven-year-olds at D.A.R.E. camp. Chung breathed relief when his mother returned alone. He loved and sometimes feared his sister. Often felt her impulses, the direction of her anger, before they surfaced. Sensed in every moment that she and his mother were a breath away from a fight. And so, though he loved Jordan, he greeted these days with hope. With release.

That first day, half-spent by her trip out of county and back, Chung's mother ordered Pizza Hut, two grease-licked cheese personals, a fat two-liter of Diet Pepsi for her, and Code Red for him.

Chung ate slowly—let the mozzarella dissolve over his tongue. He and his mother extended, stuffed every moment with all the fat that they could get. They watched all the Viggo Mortensen flicks and the Matthew McConaugheys and the Christian Bales. Chung's mother knew nothing, he supposed, about the secret well these faces filled in him, so she believed it was his kindness that allowed her to revel in them, while her daughter never stomached them. What joy he recognized in his mother, to shower herself so keenly in the things she loved. The indulgences her daughter denied her when she was near.

"Don't waste the crusts," his mother said, as Chung stood over their open-mouthed trash can. "Buddy," his mother chirped at their tawny little shih tzu, "Buddy wants some crusts, doesn't he? Don't you, baby boy, baby, baby?"

That voice his mother used. It reminded him of his earliest days, before her affection was muddied by all the years—their father's fights, the separation, his sister's fights, their inability to be apart. *Just emancipate yourself girl. Leave Chung and Buddy and me alone. We'll be better off without you.* This Mother could be hateful. His other mother, the sweet-voiced one he remembered as That Mother, existed in the sparse memories possible in his youngest years—big-gaping-mouth laughs and singing Aretha Franklin and playing detective. When they still lived on the farm and her husband had more sober moments than not.

A snap of her fingers brought Chung back to This Mother. How suddenly she shifted voices from *baby, baby boy* to *selfish, stupid girl.* She and Jordan's last hours-long fight, two weeks before, had switched on a dime like this. It started with This Mother doing the grocery shopping, which Jordan usually took care of. Their bank account was always hundreds of dollars negative, a kindness their banker allowed, but it loomed over his sister more than This or That Mother or him. If This Mother was left to do the shopping, she would come home with $300 in lottery tickets and more junk food than staples. Birthdays and holidays went the same: hundreds of dollars they didn't have, spent on gifts they didn't need. That's what Jordan would say. Chung felt similarly but also saw the wet-eyed joy it brought That Mother to give them things greater than they could expect or keep. So, two weeks ago, she did the shopping while Jordan was at a friend's house. His sister came home to a counter full of Ruffles and Ritz crackers and Cheez Whiz and soda. No bread. No milk. No fruit or vegetables or whisper of nutrition. It drove Jordan over the edge.

"They're about to close our cable account. The rent is overdue."

"You're trying to starve us," was This Mother's response, "all you ever get is healthy crap."

And somehow it ended the way all their fights did:

Jordan shouting: "I can't do this anymore. I can't."

This Mother insisting: "You're going to get Chung taken away. That's what you want. You're gonna land your little brother in foster care."

Often Chung felt sorry for his sister. Though she played as much a role as This Mother did in starting any fight they had, Jordan never bore either mothers' words with the necessary forgetfulness.

How much he had forgotten, Chung realized, looking down the throat of the trash.

"Chung," That Mother called, her edge *just* restrained. "Toss them to baby." She rolled her arm in mimicry—like the time (*how had he forgotten?*) when This Mother took their GameCube and hurled it. Like a pro. A shot-putter without the wind-up.

"Chung, you're getting that look." She drew up her hand again, ran it in a line down her face. Barely under control. Barely That Mother. He loved her but he also feared her.

"I'm fine." He dropped the crusts to the floor, and Buddy swooped in.

"Good, good baby boy," his mother purred.

THE second day they made root-beer floats and ate Cheez Whiz and watched through *Lord of the Rings,* as they had done and would do, over and over, all their years, always trudging toward Mordor and getting stranded in their descent.

Chung had shaken off the anxiety of the previous day. Discarded unwanted memories, tried his best to value their brief reprieve.

When they had finished FOTR, Chung's mother loaded *Crouching Tiger, Hidden Dragon.* In her younger years, his mother could break through three boards with one kick, splinter ribs with her fist. That Mother had been a fourth-degree black belt, a Tae Kwon Do master, a teacher. She and Chung's father owned a school for two years when Chung was four and five years old. They would spar and jump over one another's back to split wood amid a roaring audience of children, Chung and his sister among them. Those were the days when they could tussle in public and forget the source of their aches outside of the school.

Chung's mother fell asleep halfway into the movie. She had taken her medication—a growing cocktail of Clonazepam and Pristiq and pain relievers meant to dampen all those years of sparring, the shock of all those boards. Chung stayed with her through her snores, through the movie's end and longer, feeling Buddy's hot breath against his hand and reveling, for once, in their silence.

ON the third day, Chung's friend Kaleb called their landline. Asked, "Can I come over?" Chung knew it was better not to ask, his friend calling in the same manner his sister called her friends when she needed to escape, only Kaleb lived three hundred paces away, in the even shittier apartments across Fairway Drive.

"Yeah. Bring some trunks. We can swim down at the pool."

Chung's mother was an hour-deep into *Reign of Fire,* one of those blessed features offering both McConaughey and Bale, and though she overheard Chung's conversation, she didn't forbid his friend coming, as she often did. She had been friends with Kaleb's mother when they first moved, but after a year it ended up yet another bridge burned. Kaleb's mother could only stomach so many *"you're a bad influence"* gripes. Chung's mother could only look past so many *"if you had stayed married"* gibes.

At the pool Chung and Kaleb wore clingy swim trunks, both having grown since the summer before. Both without money for new pairs.

Chung knew there was never a right time to ask what was wrong, so he and his friend treaded water, took turns holding their breath, played a sad, simple game of Marco Polo.

Eventually, others came. The twin eight-year-olds from building C. The geezer from building A. The drunk, who had once touched Jordan's ass in the damp, subterrestrial laundry room the complex shared. Chung and Kaleb sat on the side of the pool, felt the coarse lip of its side, pedaled their feet. It was summer, ripe and sunbaked, and they were two preteen boys on the cusp of their first year of high school. Still, all Kaleb wanted to talk about was his mom.

"She's always staying out late like that's better than bringing her dipshit boyfriends home. She's always stealing my cigs, man." Kaleb's mother worked two minimum-wage jobs—never enough for the four of them. Kaleb had two jobs, worked child-labor-law-breaking hours by skipping class—never enough. His two younger sisters spent their summer days alone. "It just ain't right, man."

Chung listened but had no advice to offer. Never did. He watched the twins cannonball over and over, entranced, until he heard Kaleb snicker beside him. He followed his friend's stare.

Chung's mother, in her forty-nine-year-old body, in her over-washed bikini, shuffled across the pavement in bitten-through flip flops. Each step showed her years, Chung thought, and then he coughed, ashamed. His stomach soured. He focused on a leaf listing across the water.

"Get it, get it," Kaleb said, extending a high-five Chung's mother's way.

She smiled closed-lipped and tied up her hair, prickle-haired underarms untouched by the sun. She waved to another neighbor, the thirty-something mechanic from their building. The only neighbor who, though he had to have heard the many fights between his mother and sister, never knocked on their door. He smiled but didn't wave. Took the spot furthest from them.

Chung's mother shifted her swimsuit. As she stood and made her journey toward their neighbor, Chung looked away.

CHUNG and Kaleb stayed longer than anyone else. Wore their excursion on their burnt skin and chapped lips. By sunset, Chung and his friend needed hydration if they were going to stay longer. Chung headed back to his building to raid the fridge. His mother had spent an hour in the pool, her brief flirtation with their neighbor vague and harmless. Chung was thankful. He tensed at the thought of the neighbor's rejection, her humbling. He found himself suddenly aware of all his mother's vulnerabilities, spots too sore for even his sister to wield.

Chung found Buddy sleeping on the couch, which was also Chung's mother's bed. Heard the air conditioner chugging away—the only noise, he thought, with the TV black. Dead. It took him a second to catch the other tone, soft and hidden.

Chung didn't move. Knew, in a sense, that some shift had occurred in his absence. He crept to the broken room divider separating his sister's bed from the living room, knowing now, as the air conditioner sputtered off, that other pitch emanated from in there. The curve of his mother's back, prostrate, startled him. She curled on his sister's bed and didn't weep, exactly, but stifled a noise that eked out. Like the laggard breaths of the kitten Chung's mother had tried to save, back in their farm days. It was one day into this world and for all his mother's index-finger compressions and puffs of half-breath, it passed. Poor thing. No hope of life. Whenever Chung wanted to cry, knew how pointless that desire was, he remembered that little black kitten and how his tears had felt then. Weeping through memory. Hurting through ghosts.

He tiptoed back to the front door. Forgot the soda he had promised his friend and, once back at the pool and chest-deep in the water, closed his eyes, formed his mouth, strained his muscles, tried his best to call forth a specter better fit to mend them.

"You good?" Kaleb called.

Chung softened, drifted.

Open. Open. Open.

No ghost came.

DAY Four. His mother tired of the grainy texture and busted speakers of their hundred-pound TV. "What do you think?" she asked Chung, fingering the newspaper listings. Immediately, Chung spotted *Kung Fu Hustle*, that martial-arts film with the rubbery CGI and smooth choreography, as Kaleb had put it. Kaleb was an expert at appearing older than he was—buying cigarettes and full-timing and getting into R-rated movies. Sometimes, Chung envied him.

"I've heard it's good." It had been out for six weeks, and Chung was sure it would drop off the theaters any week now.

"You heard it was good? From who?"

Chung saw how he might lose her.

"It was one of Jordan's friends. She mentioned on the last bus ride before summer that it was the best movie she's seen in years."

Chung's mother nodded. "Fine, fine," she said, laying out a plate of Cheez Whiz for Buddy. They fanned their faces in the quick, baking descent to the car and blasted the AC on the five-minute drive to Salina Central Mall.

BECAUSE it was a Thursday matinee, and because the movie was in the death-crawl of its last theatrical showings, Chung and his mother found only a half-dozen other viewers peppered throughout the room. They had gotten the fixings: buttered popcorn, infant-sized drinks, and Laffy Taffy, which paired wonderfully with the salty popcorn.

Chung and his mother gleefully watched the preview teasing Cillian Murphy and Rachel McAdams' chemistry in *Red Eye*. All that promise wrapped up in one pressurized cabin. Cillian's frigid eyes. His captivating Americanized voice. That thrill buoyed Chung into *Kung Fu Hustle*'s opening music, propellant brass and a writhing string rally.

The hundredfold suit-clad Axe Gang and their suave leader, Brother Sum, terrorize a city. At their casino, Brother Sum and his thugs chant, hustle, throw their axes in the air. They are an insurmountable foe that—as a title card reads—only spare the poorest tenements from their wrath.

Chung pricked at these first violences. For all their adventure-film watching, the orange-washed Chinese Western-style of Stephen Chow felt unmatched. He observed his mother from his periphery, braced himself against her anger at the film's gore and crudity. The moment never came. She didn't frown or lean in to admonish Chung. No. She laughed as the story poured through Pigsty Alley, a gray, crowded apartment building owned by a sly, silk-pajamaed landlord and his rollered-hair and nightgown-wearing wife.

The landlady. It wasn't that she shared physical qualities with Chung's mother. But her bent posture, her cigarette-parted lips and furrowed brow, her threats to her tenants to ration water, burn down a store for late rent. Chung held back his laughs and cringed as she slapped a bare-assed buffoon and leveled her husband.

Again, Chung waited for his mother's dissatisfaction, her insistence that they leave right then and there. She simply watched the film, and so he finally did too.

Enter Sing, played by Chow, a sleazebag who fakes his way into the Axe Gang and accidentally rallies them against Pigsty Alley, only to discover that three tenants—a tailor, a baker, a laborer—are kung fu masters. Defeated, Sum hires two gray-clad zither-playing assassins. Easy, quick, they finish off the laborer. Wound the others in a masterful action scene filled with music-wrought daggers and a well-timed revelation: the landlord and landlady are also kung fu masters. The landlady's ability comes from her endless lung capacity and glass-shattering screams.

As she defeats the zither players, shreds them to their dainties, she and her husband decide enough is enough. They have a message for the Axe Gang: *Stop fucking around.*

They appear as by magic in Brother Sum's car, landlady in back, arms wrapped around Sum and his accomplice. Cigarette aloft, eyes fierce, rollers ominous, she gestures toward Sum. No more playing. Clenches her fists, cracks her knuckles. She brushes her thumb across her nose, all ferocity, power.

Chung watched all of this with exhilaration, but, against his desires, his bladder pounded. He exited the theater, relieved himself and, on his return, saw his mother's silhouette. Paused. Every part of her blue-lined shadow shook, unnerved. He didn't know if he should take his seat. He glanced at the other movie goers. Maybe he had missed something. No. Every other eye proved dry. So, he took a seat two rows back and lingered for—he didn't know what. For her to calm? For her to look for him? Now, the landlady and landlord faced down a new, enigmatic foe: the Beast, a toad-like martial artist fresh out of prison. The landlady continued her fighting, strong and quick and tireless, and finally Chung understood, he thought. Her fifty-year-old body still thrived, fought, charmed. It had been too much, seeing what might have awaited her if things had gone differently.

When his mother had stilled, he retrieved his seat next to her. Waited for her acknowledgement. It didn't come. The film ended. Chung followed his mother out of the theater. They didn't speak. Chung tensed, worried, felt guilt for his suggestion, sadness that it had hurt her in a way he hadn't anticipated.

When she turned on the car and turned off the radio, Chung braced himself.

His mother leaned over to him, eyes sharp, mouth pressed close. He thought of the farm, of their games, of her smile to steady him.

No. She waved her index finger, raised an eyebrow. She cracked her knuckles. Thumbed her nose.

Chung hesitated.

His mother smiled. Laughed. When they were halfway home, Chung noticed his mother's silenced phone alight, call incoming.

His sister.

He didn't say anything.

On their walk toward the apartment, she began her dance—smooth, natural. Hips in motion, hair bouncing. Chung, following, rallied the groove, too. Kicked his feet up the stairs. Swayed his shoulders, axe in hand.

Chung and his mother entered their apartment and pulled up the blinds. His mother grabbed their boom box and popped in Aretha. Belted. Snapped. Picked up a cheesy-faced Buddy and held him to the sun.

Chung threw off his shoes and grabbed pizza and pop and Cheez Whiz and crackers.

He could curse himself for all the ways he had shrunk her down, entertained the idea that This Mother and That Mother were two discrete identities and not one person embodying both, but for now he focused on the music, the salt and sugar coating his mouth. He summoned up the light. Closed off that gate that made him vessel, not man.

He wished, in a way, that his sister could be here, that this diversion was possible in her presence. He knew better than to hope.

And so he writhed. Though they didn't know the Hustle, they threw up their fists, wielded their axes. Rolled. Dipped. Chanted. They slicked their skin with sweat, kicked and blocked and soared.

Too soon, Chung spied blue light at the edge of his vision. Saw the flickering again of his mother's phone on the counter. He didn't stop dancing, didn't stop to think. Spied, as he expected, a number from Junction City. He hit the phone's side, caught its bright face and slid it fast, quick, quiet, into the trash.

Albuquerque

The Sister

ALBUQUERQUE

THAT Amy Badillo would throw an eighteenth birthday party better than anyone from her middle-of-a-cow-pasture school was a given. She had the money, the following, and the space. a five acre farm. Her parents, who still grew crops despite the odds, agreed to hole up in a local motel for the night so that their hedonist daughter could live out whatever last hometown dreams she desired; the appearance of freedom was their gift. Amy hadn't decided on what she wanted just yet, but she knew what people expected—that she and everybody else would get plastered, that she and everybody else would dance their asses off, and that she would probably end up on some guy's tally in the end.

Amy respected the first two expectations as honored tradition. The last one relied on who she could stomach. The majority of guys at her high school had horrific hygiene, off-brand cologne, and an ungodly obsession with either: 1. Right-wing politics (big guns) or 2. Theatre. Amy didn't know which disgusted her more.

More than anything, Amy hoped for distraction—from the looming end of her high school career, from the fact that the few kids she cared about would be moving hundreds of miles away and expected her to follow. She never pictured herself at eighteen, reluctant to attend college, to find a job, ending up yet another country girl dawdling in her hometown until she hit forty and evaporated into the air. She looked into the sky-mirrored pond of her future and felt nothing, desired nothing except to shed all knowledge of her past and present self. She had spent her life the center of attention, receiving it without effort, by her very breath. She desired a cold, clean break from everyone and everything that had defined her. Her parents, her friends, her bug-eyed little dog Fitch, all meant that any departure would be messy, hot-blooded.

As the time of the party neared, she locked herself in the bathroom, saw to the primping of every inch of her body, as if it mattered, as if anyone could turn away from her for any imperfection small or large. She painted her nails blood red, drew the markings of a mountain lion across her face, because it was nearing Halloween and all were expected to appear as something better than themselves. The first guests arrived before she was done, but she ignored them. She smudged and lined her skin to perfection, stark arches of white paint smothering her eyebrows, a dimpled pink nose masking her own. The whiskers reached across her cheeks, her jaw, clawing for her neck.

In the drawing of her face, grooming of her body, Amy finally identified the one thing that she wanted out of the night, the one thing that would mark the end of an era: to give her friends and classmates the best night of their sad, simple lives. To become selfless, charitable, if only in this memory.

JORDAN arrived with all the party favors money could buy from Party America—black and orange streamers, rubber spiders and cotton webs, a bag of dry ice. These and Jordan's presence tonight would serve as her sole birthday gifts to Amy. After what had happened the week before, Jordan was cautious to offer anything more to Amy, in case others were watching. Or Amy had lied to her, had actually taken the incident for something more serious than it was.

Again, she replayed it in her mind, as the week before they slumped into the same ripped seat on the bus ride back from district band. Jordan chose to sleep rather than spiral through the motion sickness and pubescent chatter. She didn't remember dreaming, didn't feel the passage of time, but for the sudden sweat-sodden break of her sleep. When she woke, she was alone. She sat up, craned her neck in search of Amy, only to see she had changed seats. She sat sideways on a bench two rows back as June, their only other close friend, braided Amy's hair. Amy avoided looking at her, even as Jordan leaned toward her. Instead, Jordan spied Molly Rohr gleaming at her, that twist of the mouth, the only way Molly ever addressed her now that they were ex-friends. Enemies. Days later, it was Molly who told Jordan what happened, or her version of it.

Deep asleep, Jordan had mumbled Amy's name. Everyone knew what that meant. Jordan was in love with Amy or horny for her. There was no difference between the two for the sheltered, hetero youth of central Kansas, and whether either was true didn't matter. The idea had been planted. Jordan, everyone would agree, was fucked.

Amy wouldn't be described by anyone as kind, but there was kindness in the fact that she didn't tell anyone or ever approach Jordan about the incident. Nothing more than a ripple disturbed their relationship. Perhaps one of the reasons their tiny friend group had never grown was because unlike their classmates, June, Jordan, and Amy didn't give a fuck about what people were made of. They had been spared the gays-go-to-hell vitriol of their peers' Bible-thumping parents. They had an unmatched, deep-seated love for each other, and though this love had never passed from platonic to something more, none of the girls felt the need to denounce the possibility of their being, as Molly Rohr put it, "greasy dykes, lesbo freaks, or nymphomaniacs of the clitoral variety".

Their friendship was the sole balm to Jordan's anxieties for the future. Even if college was horrible, even if she struggled to find her footing in a big city, the knowledge that Amy would be there alongside her tempered her fear. As she had learned time and time again, she and Amy could annihilate any enemy, flatten any obstacle that came their way.

If you asked Jordan, if she were really honest, she would say that she loved Amy more than she had probably loved anyone except her little brother. Homophobia didn't prevent her from sharing this, but a deep hatred for appearing weak, penetrable to others. It was Amy who had taught her the importance of appearances, of curating who saw her and how they saw her. That's why, given the timing of the party and her need to alter herself, she came to the party dressed not as prey, but predator. She arrived donning a pair of brown-gray ears, a snout, and fangs.

"Wolf?" Amy asked.

"Coyote."

There were no wolves in Kansas, but coyotes hid in every abandoned shed, every shallow burrow and unsuspecting farmer's tractor bed, those rare, solitary coyotes just looking for a warm place to sleep, and the farmers, always an arm's grab away from a shotgun.

Amy poured Jordan a glass of OJ, one of the girls' many silent affirmations of affection. Everybody else would be drinking screwdrivers, vodka and orange juice, and Amy knew the juice would disguise Jordan's decision not to drink—something worthy of ridicule in their little patch of prairie. Jordan, conscious of the century-long legacy of alcoholism in her family, wasn't keen on tempting fate. She hadn't had a sip of alcohol ever in her life. At least not intentionally. She would never forgive Matt Rohr for tricking her into drinking his heinous cocktail all those years ago.

"Thank you, babe," Amy said, acknowledging the plastic bags stuffed full of decorations. "Help me get those up before Molly starts bitching about how lame this is going to be."

Their high school consisted of less than three hundred people, and only fifty of those sad, weed-patch-dwelling losers ever showed up to party. Jordan got a fire going and June, dressed as as a Sexy Bo Peep, dispensed the drinks. Amy made her entrance once everyone had settled down on overturned buckets, dead logs, or the nail-mixed gravel of her parents' driveway. It was easy, holding their attention, lighting a match in a cold, dark cave.

Amy took a seat on the stump of an old oak tree her parents had never dug up. Jordan sat next to June, the former always reluctant to meet new people at parties, the latter always looking to expand her friend group. This proximity meant Jordan could sit in silence, undisturbed.

The festivities began with a round of ghost stories. John Wesley and Molly and Matt Rohr were there, even though John and Matt had already graduated. Everyone but Jordan accepted the vodka and OJ cups June handed out. Someone brought the fixings for s'mores, and so Amy's mother's closet was raided for hangers that were then unbent into wavy spears, ready to impale.

After the first few stories, half the group broke off, including Amy and June, for a game of spin-the-bottle. Jordan stayed and stewed around the fire, because she wasn't about to kiss any oily dumbasses from her class. None of them seemed to brush their teeth on the regular.

Matt Rohr was still among the bonfire group, and Jordan was keen to keep her distance. He had always badgered her in school and on the rare occasion she spent a night at the Rohrs' house, until Molly dropped Jordan as a friend.

A flashing speck of ash landed on Jordan's knee. She snuffed it out with her palm and stabbed three marshmallows onto her wire. She twirled it near the cinders where the best heat was, and just as she stuck one of those deliciously crispy things in her mouth, a boy, bloodied and crusted with dirt, took the seat next to her.

"Wolf?" the boy asked, pointing to her costume.

"Coyote."

"Appropriate," the bloodied boy said.

"Because?"

"You look ready to bite someone's head off," he said.

The boy couldn't have been more than twenty, and she had never seen him before. She assumed he was Amy's cousin. He looked like her a little.

"What are you supposed to be, roadkill?" Jordan stuffed another marshmallow in her mouth. She hoped the boy would take a hint and find another seat. Instead, he picked up a hanger and sanitized it in the fire.

"Are you friends with the birthday girl?" the boy asked, ignoring Jordan's glaring disinterest in him. "Or did you just wander out of the woods. I don't mind party crashers, myself. Won't tell anyone. I swear."

Jordan got up and headed toward the spin-the-bottle group. She forgot her Solo cup back at the bonfire. She asked Amy if she had any games they could break out, something to save her from forced conversations.

"No one wants to play cards," Amy said.

"Are you kidding? I mean, strip poker?" one of the boys called, but the girls ignored him.

Amy curled her torso toward Jordan and bunched up her shoulders, an obvious move to show off her boobs, to Jordan and everyone else.

"Just sit down and play with us," Amy replied. "We're doing no-holds-barred. Guys smooching guys, et cetera."

All the group laughed.

Did they know? Had Amy told the whole fucking school about that one faceless dream? Jordan couldn't believe it, couldn't believe her friend would turn on her so abruptly, so stupidly, and yet Amy's throaty chuckle was among the noise.

Fuck her. Fuck them. Fuck this stupid sleeping brain for betraying me. Jordan went back to the fire and took a long gulp of her drink. She had swallowed half the cup when she realized it was wrong. Her throat stung.

She felt nauseous. She had drunk the wrong cup, or someone had spiked hers with vodka. Like that, she flashed back, images of her father, his shattered glass and torn skin and acrid stomach acid spilled across the carpet of her parents' bedroom. Her mother, who refused to clean it up. Her father who would wake ten hours later, crying, convinced he had suffocated them all, but it had only been a dream.

Jordan ran into the house and into the bathroom where she made herself spit all of it up. And still, her throat screamed. Her world shivered.

AMY actually hated spin-the-bottle. She preferred not to trust the faulty physics of the bottle on uneven grass. Almost always, she ended up kissing the one person she didn't want to acknowledge, let alone swap spit with.

She felt guilty, teasing Jordan in front of everyone for something she herself had no issue with. She hadn't told anyone about the dream. She had simply moved seats to sit with June, who braided her hair without tugging too hard—Jordan always left her scalp burning. It had been Molly Rohr, Amy knew. Molly had it out for Jordan after she had called her brother a waste of breath, after she had pushed him down the stairs and left him for dead (though Amy remembered Jordan's side of the story; that Matt had blocked her on that stairwell, tried to pull her up to his bedroom). Molly had spread rumors, snuck dead mice into Jordan's locker and called her a witch, and when that didn't take, an asexual freak, and when that didn't take, she spit the word lesbian all around the school, the country, the internet.

If it had been Amy, the damage would've been irreversible.

As the game went on and she spun, turn after turn, always landing on some flimsy-ass boy, Amy soured against the whole thing. When Matt Rohr finally joined the group and began making eyes at her, she considered suffocating the bonfire and locking herself up in her house until everybody was long gone. The whole idea, of granting everybody the best night of their lives, paled after Jordan had stormed off. All the painted faces around her felt like no more than cruel accomplices in her friend's unhappiness. She needed to make it right.

Amy proposed a break in the game. She needed to pee, she said, but really she needed to swallow a few more fingers of McCormick's before she approached her flammable friend.

As Amy searched the house, her limbs vibrated from the vodka. Upstairs, she spied the bathroom door open, someone inside. Pushing it open, Amy found Jordan rubbing toothpaste over her teeth. Amy's toothpaste.

For a moment the girls didn't say anything. Jordan stared at her, mouth all foam, eyes wide. Amy didn't know what to make of it, except that it was possible that maybe she had underestimated Jordan's infatuation with her. She backed out into the hallway, all looks and no words. She sucked when it came to apologies. She didn't know how to make them sound sincere. Instead, Jordan was the first to apologize.

"Sorry," Jordan said after rinsing out her mouth.

"Don't worry about it." Amy was already in the bathroom again, stripping off her jeans to squat over the toilet. Jordan, mouth still ringed with white foam, stepped out of the room and shut the door.

AT the bottom of the stairs, Jordan found Molly Rohr and John Wesley making out in the kitchen. She slinked into the living room. She scanned her eyes over the Badillo collection of board and card games, still desperate for some less-bawdy activity to occupy her time. It was her duty, as a friend, to be here. To leave early would be a smack in the face.

"Don't bite," a voice said, approaching from behind. It was the bloodied boy. "Woah, rabies?"

Jordan remembered the toothpaste drying over her mouth. She wiped it away with her sleeve.

"The last boy who wouldn't leave me alone ended up at the bottom of the stairs. Hasn't walked the same since."

"That's not true," the boy said.

A toilet flushed upstairs, and Amy glided down the stairs, smacking her lips over a fresh layer of lipstick. She didn't pay any attention to the boy or Jordan but walked straight outside.

"How do you know Amy again?" Jordan asked.

The boy lifted a box, The Game of Life, and handed it to Jordan.

"No. Hate it."

In the soft domestic light, the boy proved to be acceptably handsome. Built like a runner, all calves. He had a mean farmer's tan which, for

October, made him more than your seasonal harvester. He worked with his hands.

"How would you describe me?" Jordan was looking for honesty because the best lies came from the keenest truth-tellers.

"In one word? Scary." He smiled and his canines flashed gold in the warm light. "In two words: Self-denying."

"Because?" Jordan had expected the first. The second surprised her.

"You dressed up as a coyote instead of a wolf, for one. A lesser predator. You seem content following your grenade of a friend, instead of commanding the attention you deserve—"

"Thanks for trying. I'll find somebody else."

"—and you believe that your only way forward is to be alone. You don't have friends. You have placeholders, temporary and insignificant."

"I would murder for my friends," she said, as a fact and a warning.

"You would murder for that ditzy shepherdess?"

"June isn't ditzy, she just acts that way so people leave her alone. People like you."

The truth was that Jordan wouldn't necessarily murder someone for June, but she'd definitely make them crawl through the end of their days. If it were Amy who needed avenging, Jordan knew torture would be more appropriate than a quick death.

"You started quizzing me. I'm just curious." The boy picked out the game Sorry.

Jordan swatted it out of his hand, and the pieces scattered.

"Have fun," she said, before returning to the party outside.

WHAT Amy found on her re-entry to the party was a verified snoozer. The bonfire had flickered out. The kissing game had been abandoned. People broke off into groups and took turns turning joints to ash and ripping apart the grass under their feet. Amy's brain—rattled by the toothpaste sharing and the appearance of Jordan consorting with some guy she hadn't seen before—rooted for distraction. She needed to act fast. First, she brought out her boom box and blared Ciara until a few drunkards began dancing around the non-fire. She gathered more sticks and brush to bring the bonfire back to life. When enough people were dancing she joined in, putting on the sort of show lechers would toss up a few hundreds for, just to extend the glamor a little longer.

She had to fight off Matt Rohr (who had the audacity to approach her from behind) and slip away from another boy who was dressed up in all Confederate-flag clothing. John Wesley showed an interest, but Amy wasn't sure yet if she could dominate Molly in the inevitable fight. She was still dancing by herself when Jordan exited the house.

"Jordan," Amy shouted, dizzy from the movement and looking for an anchor. She hooked her finger and beckoned Jordan to join her. Did her best hair flip and puckered lip, just enough to get the others laughing, which hadn't been her intention. It was always how she tried to rope Jordan into dancing, which Jordan never did.

Molly appeared out of some dark corner of the farm and pointed her finger at Jordan. "Hey queer baby, show us what a lesbo dances like. Is it all hips or just head-bobbing for you fuckers?"

Amy should've stopped dancing then, because she didn't want to ridicule Jordan. She just wanted another warm body.

Eventually, a boy emerged from the farmhouse, whispered in Jordan's ear, and led her off to some lightless patch of earth. Amy threw her cup into the fire and grabbed the nearest handle and went inside. The orange light, the hard-cut stairs all greeted her in hexagonal glory. The floorboards' creaks signaled to her that she was on the right path. After some struggle, she made it to her bedroom. Climbed into her bed. She found her shih-tzu, Fitch, lying under her comforter and curled her body around his.

If Amy was honest, Jordan was a closer friend to her than anyone else. Jordan wasn't like anyone she knew. She told you upfront what she thought of you or your feckless boyfriends or your hideous dog.

Amy listened to Fitch's wheezing, felt the vibration of his little ribs against hers. He was pretty hideous, but like Jordan also knew, was just as beautiful in his grotesquerie as any other living thing. This was something else Amy liked about Jordan. She could be brutal and shut-off from people, but she god-damn loved every animal on this planet. And it was through this love that she allotted humans their imperfections, too.

With the heat of his compact dog body against hers, Amy lulled herself into a deep sleep. She didn't dream. When she woke, a thick brown haze had settled into her room, swept in from her open bedroom window.

"NEED a lifeline?" the bloodied boy had asked Jordan when he caught up with her again outside. "That's what you want, right? To get them off your tail."

"I don't need your help—" she said, though actually, she had thought to ask the boy for his help inside, then thought better of it, and decided instead to knock the game from his hands because she didn't think she could trust him. But now that Molly crept out of the shadows to bad-mouth her, Jordan reconsidered. Sure, she had weathered harsher words from her mother than Molly Rohr could ever cough up, but—"but okay. Fine."

They wound through the thin woods circling the farm. It was a moonless night, so they tripped over uprooted trees and thorny bushes.

"Did you spike my drink?" she asked, when they were free of the others. Jordan had been sitting on the question since it had happened.

"How could you spike a screwdriver? It's already fifty percent vodka."

"You were sitting right there when I left my spot. You weren't there when I came back."

The boy said he didn't; he wasn't that desperate, he wasn't that much of a loser, and Jordan believed him. He didn't seem like the kind of desperate that resorted to sneaking alcohol into a girl's orange juice. His persistence posed a problem to her because she couldn't place why he kept showing up, following her, but she wasn't worried. She could kick him in the nuts or scream or run back to the farm, easy. And there was always that old trick of hers: her smoke. All she had to do was dredge up some old hurt, stoke her anger until it came rushing out of her. It always stopped others in their tracks.

"How long should we fake-canoodle? An hour?" the boy sat on a flat patch of prairie grass and Jordan rested nearby, just out of arm's reach.

Now that she was away from Amy and everyone else, Jordan realized there was no reason to go back. She could sneak to her car and drive off, sending gravel dust high into the black and windless October air.

"Where are you going?"

Jordan knew that staying there any longer would just be giving fuel to Molly and the other assholes' fire. Now that Amy had abandoned the charity she'd granted Jordan over the last few days. Now that Jordan was just a joke. And to be perfectly honest, Jordan did find Amy attractive. Of course she did; everyone did. And Jordan and Amy had been friends since sixth grade. Over the five years of their friendship, Amy had transformed Jordan from a brooding doormat into a contemptuous bitch. If Jordan hadn't slipped up in her sleep and Molly or whoever hadn't told everyone at school, then who knew. Jordan might not have found herself turned away from the prospect. Still, she couldn't remember the dream.

"Hey. Walking off like that. You really forget other people are around you." The boy trailed behind her as she headed back to the farm, choosing an alternative route that led her closer to her car, away from the crowd. He caught up to her side, "If we go back this early, they won't buy it."

"I'm going home." She stopped at the back of the farmhouse and peered around, looking for stragglers who might announce her departure. "It sure was a pleasure."

"Don't just leave." He touched Jordan's arm, and usually she would have shaken him off, but she was too tired. Maybe it was the droplets of vodka still slogging through her system. Maybe it was the feeling that her friendship with Amy was terminal. She couldn't move.

"Instead of leaving," the boy said, sliding up to her front, "what if we did something else. Something to really make them regret their little jokes."

"What are you doing? I don't even know you."

"I have an idea."

"I don't care." Jordan moved around him.

"They think you'll take their jokes lying down. Why don't you send them running for the hills?" The bloodied boy pulled a lighter out of his pocket and flicked it alive. He smiled.

Jordan paused. Glanced around her shoulder at her car. She had been the kind of person to slink off and leave this world behind before she met Amy. No, now, she knew she couldn't back track. She had come so far.

Creeping around the back of the house, the bloodied boy and Jordan approached the old-fashioned red-painted barn that housed rotting hay bales and rusted-out equipment. A few of the Badillo's old outdoor dogs rested there, and Jordan was careful to lead them outside before sliding the door shut.

The boy began clearing the dirt floor of debris to stack a small mound of hay on the earth, but Jordan stopped him.

"That won't be necessary," she said, taking a deep breath. Feeding her fire.

"What? I thought you were down for this."

"We don't need any of that."

Still the boy didn't understand, and Jordan didn't care enough to explain it to him. Instead, she conjured up her smoke, thought of Molly's laughter and Amy's probing.

Thick as water, it poured out of her. The boy muttered a "what-the-fuck," and stepped back, but Jordan saw the fire in his eyes. She stoked and stoked her fumes until they funneled out of the open barn window above them and hung over the party.

The boy gave her one last smile before opening a side door and running out.

"Fire! Fire! Run!" he screamed, a convincing fake.

When the fools had scattered, screaming, too, the boy returned to Jordan. Told her how gorgeous she was. What was she? A witch, a real one? She was amazing. Jordan shivered.

She kissed him and led him back into the moonless woods, promising no curses awaited him there.

AMY had slept through the noise. As she stepped out onto the porch of the house, the driveway lay deserted. Most of the party had driven off in their hysteria, leaving behind overturned cups and open handles, glugging their contents onto the quenched earth. Amy found June making out with John Wesley behind a tree. She pulled June by the pigtails until the girl told her everything. The two girls inspected the barn to find nothing. No sign of a fire started there. No sign of charred wood around the loft window sill. Only then did they know for sure that it had been Jordan, her little magic. But before Amy could feel anger or sadness or relief, she saw Jordan and the bloodied boy walking out of the woods, still buttoning their shirts.

"What the hell," Amy said, deciding to be angry only because she didn't know how else to proceed.

"Did something happen?" the boy asked. "We heard the shouting but were . . . . pre-occupied."

Jordan headed straight toward her car.

"Why would you do that?" Amy said.

"A little smoke? You and I have made worse." Jordan avoided her.

"No," Amy said, stomping up to her. "Why would you sleep with a loser like him?"

And Jordan took this to mean that Amy *knew* the boy. *Perhaps they are cousins? Maybe more? Who cares.* She shook her car key free and reached for the driver-side door until Amy smacked her palm against its glass.

Jordan stood her ground, "Why would you play up a theory we all know isn't true?" she asked, and in her face Amy saw that she was angry for real, livid and still somehow suppressing that emission of hers.

Amy hadn't meant to stir the shit. In fact, she had meant to apologize, despite their little prank. Jordan's friendship was the one thing keeping Amy from wanting to abandon everything and make a new life somewhere far away, like Albuquerque, somewhere brown and boiling and willing to ignore a girl like her. She had grown tired of men's blip of interest in her. She needed somewhere to plant her roots, to forget this backwater for drier fields. She had accepted an offer from a Kansas college, told Jordan they would be going together, but she knew she wouldn't be following through with it.

Amy knew she should apologize, but she also knew it wouldn't be enough. The damage had been done, and because she had bought into the fun, no one would ever believe Jordan again. She doomed her friend to end out her senior year as the school freak, and no amount of dirt-throwing would save her from it.

"Jordan," she said, refusing to let her open the car door. Still, she thought to apologize, but the right words wouldn't come to her.

Jordan, irritated, glanced back at the boy.

"How do you know him?"

"I don't know him," Amy said, watching the boy turn around and step back into the woods.

When Jordan didn't say anything, didn't seem to care that the boy had walked off, Amy asked what the guy's name was.

How would she know? She didn't care to ask.

JORDAN could almost see red flaring up in the whites of Amy's eyes, and for a second she felt guilty. Some birthday party, she wanted to say. But she was still singed by Amy's betrayal. "I'm guessing you didn't get any," Jordan said instead, but before she could try again, Amy was leaning in, breath foul with alcohol, and Jordan couldn't tell whether it was real or another joke, so she dipped away. Managed to open her driver-side door and close it behind her before Amy could try anything else.

Fuck her, Jordan thought. *Fuck her, fuck her, fuck her to the lightless moon and back.* As she drove down the long gravel roads leading back to Salina, she didn't bother with headlights; the glow of the town provided her only guiding light. Just beyond, the world teemed and waited, backs arched. She rolled down her windows and sucked in the raw air of the country. She let fly her mask and ears, rubbing the cheap face paint from her skin until all her blood collected right under the surface—she looked at herself in the rearview mirror, all off-color and jagged, and it was only then that Jordan remembered her dream.

THEY are together. On the road. Leaning into the curves, the shoulder. Their voices like waves. Like so many dreams before. It's the water. And just them. Two girls. Strong swimmers. They swim in an ocean of luminescent golds and greens and blues and purples, waves that fight for the sky but crash like pillows to a bed. They dive deep and come up no more starved of breath than marathoners on their first mile. For days and days, Amy and Jordan churn like this, content to search the complicated seafloor and then welcome the blinding sun in turns. It is glory. Just them. Breaking free. Unfettered serenity. But just as they recognize that—that they could make something of their own, of a grand, glowing world, Amy dips away, all comfort and beauty suddenly stripped away by the will of the water. The rip current sweeps her, with all the others, and in their place a massive orca, as big as a raft, as a school bus, but colorless, that sings for Jordan, still sings, such a lament that, had she remembered her dream earlier, she might never have awakened again.

THE effect, for Jordan, was lessened now against the freezing loneliness of the night. As she approached the town, its lights meant to coax her, to carry her back. What was home anyway? Instead, she pulled off to the shoulder, switched off her lights, and slept. She was so, so tired. She slept shallowly, heatless sweat collecting in every pit and peak of her, but in the morning she woke to a sea of fire, brilliant grass reflecting the sun. The anger of the night before bleached against its rays, and Jordan knew she need only apologize, forgive, and all would be rectified. She started the ignition, rounded the road, and headed back to Amy.

*W*HEN June and John Wesley had finally left (together) that night, and Amy was finally and truly alone, she ran a bath. Filled the steaming water to the rim so that her displacement would be a messy one. The heat numbed whatever nerves hadn't been dulled by the vodka. She took turns slapping her thighs and her arms under the water, the liquid sloshing over the sides and dissolving from her world.

When the silent sweep of dawn crept across the settled bathwater, Amy thought of that dreamland. Albuquerque. She imagined what her life there could be. A still pond; herself, a dropped pebble sending minute ripples across the surface, until, like everything else, she faded into the static. Thinking of that place buoyed her for a moment, until she heard the crunch and swoosh of gravel near, the murmur of that familiar car, that reality too big for her, that unknown ocean her pond was meant to forestall, and she knew that there was no going anywhere, no dreaming but of her.

Warm Lines, Cold Shadows

Warm Lines, Cold Shadows

The Brother

WARM LINES, COLD SHADOWS

1. USES

I'M the last one they tell. It's the day of, when Uncle Sunny and our aunts, Jane and Dahlia, are already lifting off the tarmac in LA, landing in Kansas City, driving three hours west to our city which is a small town to anyone else in the world. "We all know you can't lie," Mom says. I tell her she's given me no time to shop. I'm supposed to show up to a secret Christmas dinner with empty arms so that my grandma's heart breaks, and my other aunt and her daughter think me even more ungrateful/leeching than every other day.

"Just put your name on mine," Jordan says, like she isn't the worst gift giver in the family. No one wants a book they've never heard of and will never read.

The dinner will take place at my dad's parent's house in town, not the farm where his sister, my aunt, lives—where my sister and I spent our young lives before all the crops failed and our parents split, and our father wrecked his truck and then went to rehab and then relapsed and moved cross-county to a one-bedroom house with a busted heater and cobweb corners. He's the reason we're not having the family Christmas at the farm. There's no keeping it from him if we get together there. He always crawls by, weepy, when he's drunk, and given he's spending Christmas alone, that excursion is certain.

When they tell me about the dinner, tell me to lie, I consider driving over to Dad's tiny, spidery home and spending Christmas Eve with him. I don't have to say anything about the dinner, just make up for the cruelty of my grandparents and aunts and uncle and mother.

"This might be the last time you get to see your grandma," Mom says, though our paternal grandmother is only seventy-five and made of sturdy German stock and in better health than most. But Mom is allowed to dream.

In our grandparents' living room, my sister and I laugh in response to our grandfather's jokes, which we've heard before, and accept the kissed cheeks our grandmother gives, finally, after so many years of muted warmth. In her seventies, she has gotten past her aversion to affection, to telling us she loves us. She hugs us now. I am still in my own nauseated phase and so I pull away earlier than I should. Jordan holds tight for too long. She's left for college recently and whether it was there or during the summer before, someone or something broke her heart, twisted her inside, so she's holding on to everything, everyone, just a little past normal.

Grandma leads us to her basement, where our red-haired aunt and her rabbit-faced daughter, my cousin, are at work logging Grandma into Facebook, a website she neither understands nor uses except to keep tabs on us.

"Chung," my cousin, all buck teeth and freckles, calls. "You're the youngest. You should know how to do this."

I do, and I get them in after one attempt.

"See, I knew you had a use for something," she says, all squinting eyes and oversized ears.

In the kitchen, Mom whispers to Grandpa and we can guess about what. *He won't turn around if we don't cut him off.* That was her advice the last time the four of us were in a room together. Jordan had huffed because she was tired of their plans for him. My face had reddened but I couldn't say a thing. My mouth, a gaping black hole. Like our goldfish. *Glug glug glug.* Nothing.

It wasn't Mom's idea, leaving our father out this Christmas. It was his sister's. She's the only ginger in the family, our aunt. I think that's why she's always trying to make a point. To insist she has a soul, a mind of her own. It doesn't help that this is the first Christmas our mother's siblings are flying in from L.A. since they—for whatever reason, there are plenty—wrote our father off. Refused to come back while he was around.

"Can you get the wreath for your frail, old Grandpa?" our grandfather asks me, because he's near six foot and his back is bad and I am small and short (shorter even than Jordan) and can reach the back of the closet like no one else. *My little Pinocchio* Jordan used to call me, when our difference in size was more drastic.

The wreath, because our grandparents respect, maybe even fear, Mom's siblings who are all half-Korean (like our mother) and well off and more stable than our mother (who is always calling our grandparents, showing up on their doorstep asking for a loan or a reference or an answer to her latest conspiracy about them and their son—did you cut the brake line on my car? did you tell that manager I was crazy? did you or your son steal my house key and make copies?).

It didn't help that that last one was actually true.

I have just balanced the wreath on a nail over our grandparent's front door when a golden hand wraps around my shoulder. Sunny.

"Bubba," aunt Dahlia, the youngest and shortest of the three, sings as she hugs me. "You've grown," she says. I'm taller than her now, which is something, but given that I'm sixteen I'm unlikely to grow again. Jane hands me her purse, because they've been driving so long and she's fading, she needs a martini, and I have to remind her this dinner is dry. All of our family dinners have been for as long as I can remember. Sunny removes his hand and holds the door for us and in the soft light of my grandparents' home says how nice it is to be on familiar ground again.

"Cut the line," I find my mother saying in the kitchen to no one.

In the basement bathroom, my sister cries where she thinks no one will hear her.

My cousin smokes a joint in the backyard and offers it to me. "Don't worry, it's free."

Soon, Sunny, Jane, and Dahlia stretch out on the back porch, absorbing the winter sun and blessing the chill and passing their own joint between their lips like what we've come for is one thing and not too many to name.

2. EVERYTHING

OUR grandparent's house rests on the north end of the Hill, the rich (but not too rich) neighborhood of our small city/big town. Our grandparents were successful as farmers, before my sister or I were born, and so they have been able to offer my parents the farm, and when our parents failed at that, a house for Dad and a car for Mom. What brought our grandparents wealth and happiness wrought my parents financial ruin and a violent, loud separation. Now, she is sober and he is not, though whether she is better sober is up for debate. At least when she was zoned out on clonazepam she didn't spend her days spinning theories about how everyone in her life was trying to kill her. I am the lone exception to her delusion because she thinks I am incapable of killing anything.

I think she's right.

Grandma and my aunt begin the cooking. Jordan surfaces thirty minutes after she disappeared to the basement, and she's waited long enough that her eyes are white and skin less raw. Our cousin is stoned out of her mind until I bring her the crackers and cheese ball Grandma always makes, and my cousin takes her big front teeth and buries them right into the ball. I decide not to tell anyone when I bring the plate back—the cream cheese, cheddar, green onion, and pecan mass cratered now—how my cousin has tainted this good thing, because even though she rarely grants me grace, I can't return her contempt.

It is in the cooking that Grandma and my aunt realize they are missing not one but many ingredients. Kidney beans and green peppers for the chili. Yeast for the cinnamon rolls. The ground beef has turned, and the onion is molded. Overnight, ingredients have spoiled, some unseen rot tainting them. My ginger aunt asks us kids to fetch everything they need. *Everything?* I want to ask her, because there's no hope for that, but instead Jordan drives, and our cousin curls up in the backseat and I turn on the radio.

The grocery store is closing at three for the holiday, and we make it just in time. Jordan holds the basket, because our cousin has stayed in the car and my arms are weak—my left, from the time Dad drunkenly backed the tractor into the shed I was playing in and broke my forearm bones in three places; my right is perpetually locking up, probably traumatized from the time the riding mower Dad and I rode tipped over and pinned us until Jordan and Mom finally heard us and set us free.

We're in the produce section when I realize it's not unlikely Dad could run into us here. I tug on Jordan's unimpeded arm. I whisper, *We should get out of here.* In his post-rehab days before he abandoned the farm, he was always stopping at this grocery store before he'd drive us to the farm for his court-mandated weekends. Like treasures could be found here that would dull his mistakes, make up for him showing up drunk to our baseball or volleyball games or ending up in the ER the day of our graduation.

"What if he runs into us here?" I ask her as she shrugs me off and leads us down a busy aisle.

"He won't," she says, blessed with certainty.

Our cousin has finally crested past the flood when we return to the car. Her eyes, too, wane white from the scorched red they were half an hour ago. She's a year above me, two years younger than Jordan. She goes to school in Solomon and her mother rarely brings her up to Salina, except when Grandma calls and begs, in her old-age clarity, for a little relief from her loneliness. Our mother never lets us visit them, though in Jordan's post-high school freedom she goes whenever she wants and takes me with her.

The college Jordan chose is two hours east of here, in an even bigger not-city, three times the size of here. In her first semester, she has (in her own words) learned how to read people. Predator or prey. Does she miss Salina? I asked her on her first visit back. She laughed. What is there to miss except pain? In her little-big college town, there are faces she's never seen before. In one of them, she's sure, is someone incapable of hurting her.

When we return, our mother is the one in the basement doing God knows what, and Jane, Dahlia, and Sunny are in the kitchen chopping vegetables and filling the house with aromas too grandiose for this selfish thing we're doing, fencing out my father so we can have a semblance of normalcy.

Jane has snuck in vodka, we know now, because we catch her pouring a one-ounce bottle into her tea as we walk in. Sunny salts the beef we've brought. Dahlia washes the green peppers and plops the diced onion in a bowl of ice water. Such a good soul she is, saving us our tears.

"Your Grandma needed a break," Dahlia says, layering the onion over the sizzling beef. "She's had a long day."

"So have we," Jane replies, all red cheeks and grumbling, because she hates flying and hates driving cross-country, and now she's having to work to make this dinner happen and fake sobriety to save face.

Dahlia touches my arm. "Chung, get your mom, won't you? She's the best at kneading dough." Tough knuckles, our father would say, from our mother's days as a Tae Kwon Do instructor. Now, nerves up and down her spine rouse at the slightest labor. Maybe it was the mixture of pain pills and the clonazepam that did it. Made her incapable of experiencing the world like the rest of us.

The bathroom door is unlocked when I open it. My mother is sitting in the dry bathtub, fully clothed, sniffing each of the shampoo/body wash/conditioner bottles found there.

"Everything okay?" I ask her, as if she welcomes that question. She throws the bottles down. She stands and stares at me.

"Yeah. You?" Hands on hips, her ass splotched wet from the tub's remaining drops.

"Yeah," I say, stepping out of the room. "They want you to help with the rolls."

"Alright," she says, surveying the room before she leaves, like she's got to memorize how things are for when she comes back.

3. SMOKE SCREEN

IN the backyard, Jordan and our cousin huddle together, freckled faces close, breath between them one icy cloud. Both pairs of eyes wax pink, both spines curve and tilt, drawn by tense muscles, prepared for impact. When they see me they smile and scoot to make room, like what they're conjuring has a place for me, too, but instead of an explanation they are silent, both padding their feet on the frozen grass and searching the sky for any topic other than what's just been dropped.

I think to check on Grandma, whose own back has been fortified with metal and fused and sutured and still brings her so much pain, but I don't.

In the living room, I sit and count the Christmas tree needles. So many have fallen to the carpet and still it fills up the room, looms behemoth.

THE last time I visited Dad's house was toward the end of summer when a wildfire was eating away pasture ten miles west of him and his basement had flooded yet again, rendering the whole miniature house one humid, smoky mess. I went alone, because Jordan was off attending college orientation. Mom dropped me off, because though I had a license and a car at the time (made possible by Grandma and Grandpa), she insisted on driving, probably because she wanted to see the house, gauge from its exterior whether our father was up to anything he shouldn't be.

Those were her less paranoid days. To be honest, I don't know what sparked her recent spiral, though I have my guesses (her short-term boyfriend suddenly dumping her; her boss at the used-car dealership cutting her hours in half; our little dog, Buddy, dying while we were out getting groceries).

Dad didn't make the usual attempt to hide his drinking. There were opened Bud Light bottles all around the living room and rolling off the trash can, and the fridge was thoroughly stocked with more and little else. Half the lights in the house were burnt out. He wasn't drunk when I arrived, and he didn't touch beer for the remainder of the day. We sat on the cement-block porch facing west, facing the smoke, just perceptible against the slate of the sky, a slowing storm. Eventually, the rain caught up with us, dotted the gravel driveway leading back to civilization. As the ground muddied and the air became flush with electricity, a small gray cat with three legs darted through the prairie grass, leapt onto the porch and straight into my dad's lap.

"My little friend," he said, meeting the kitten's butting head with his hand. The cat emitted its own thunder and found refuge under his open coat. "I call him Bubba."

Over the last few years, Jordan and I had spent less and less time at Dad's house. If we saw him, it was more often meeting in town at the mall or Bogey's or catching a movie. I couldn't think of more than a handful of times we'd seen him over the last year, and so of course I registered why the cat had my nickname, why he had stopped grooming his house to hide the truth.

The rain turned torrential and so we rushed inside, Bubba hopping ahead of us. Dad turned on the TV and ordered Domino's and asked me what I wanted to watch, and we settled on an old VHS of *Unforgiven*. I expected Bubba to come to me at some point, but the thing stuck with Dad the whole afternoon, tucked tight against his stomach. I should've been concerned, with the bottles and the darkness and the disorder he surrounded himself with, but instead I felt relief. He was no longer fighting it. We watched another Western when the first ended, and in the morning he drove me back to Mom's apartment.

"Come back whenever you want," he said as I touched pavement again. "Don't have to call, just stop by whenever you want."

For whatever reason, I haven't gone back.

WE do the gift giving before dinner, because the chili needs its time to thicken and the rolls time to balloon. We let our grandmother rest, because she isn't ready, and, like always, I'm tasked with picking up each present and depositing them in the lap of the receiver. Each round, I bend and rub against the tree and add more needles to my hair. Each mountain (or hill) of boxes or bags or shapeless wrapped lumps is left untouched until I sit down on my grandmother's couch next to Jordan and she wipes the prickling needles from my hair.

Jordan gets a blanket with her college's mascot, a mystical bird, plastered over the front. Jane, Sunny, and Dahlia gift her a notebook set, because she wants to be a writer. My cousin receives a makeup set and a dress and overlarge earrings. Mom gets money and a self-help book thinly veiled as memoir and a coffee mug with World's Best Mom on the front (from her siblings, not her children). Grandma and Grandpa get the same as every year: slippers, more coffee mugs, and handwritten cards from everyone but me.

I'm the last to open gifts.

"Do the big one first," Jane says, all smiles now. "It's from us." She tries to wink but ends up blinking both eyes.

Inside the big one: a generic artist's case, including colored pencils, multi-colored markers, pastels, and pencils. The kind of cheap art materials that are great for gestures and little else. Still, I thank them, because unlike Mom they see merit in my creating. Always, they like the photos of drawings I post to Facebook. Always, they comment with exaggerated compliments, all the positive emojis to be found.

"Thank you," I say.

Satisfied, Jane gets up to check on the food.

Our grandparents hand me money, and Mom and Jordan have bought me a new set of sweaters.

"And ours," my cousin replies, pointing to the smallest bag.

Inside the smallest bag: an electric shaver and a smoky cologne.

Hair has just begun to pepper my chin. The cologne, I think, is to mask my sister's smoke when she's around. Or to make me more like her. Strange. Deviant.

"Chili's ready," Jane calls from the kitchen. Sunny and Dahlia push me to the front of the line, everyone always eager that I get my fill first, and my cousin lingers at the back, cutting the air with her smile. "Leave some for the rest of us," she says before I've touched a single thing. That backyard tryst ebbs away and we're back to our bickering selves.

"Take everything you want," Jordan rebuts, reaching around me and slipping a whole cinnamon roll into her mouth.

4. GRACE

SALTINES. Shredded cheddar. Sour Cream. Fritos. We have all the fixings and still Mom spends ten minutes looking for nameless ingredients and everyone forgets to tell Grandma dinner has started and Jane has forgone hiding her drinking and empties another vodka bottle into her tea. Grandma surfaces just before my cousin sits down, and we all pretend like we were letting her rest until the very last moment. Her eyes, like my sister and cousin before her, wear a tinge of red.

Grandpa says Grace and Jordan and I pretend we're listening, transmitting our grandfather's message to the heavens. Dahlia and Sunny ask me once, twice, three times if there's anything else I need, if we're missing anything, before finally I convince them I'm good, remind them that their own bowls will go cold if they don't hurry up and enjoy them already.

Just when we're all settled in: a knock at the door.

And then: my cousin gets up. Checks the door, which isn't far from us now, just a hallway away.

Quiet murmurs and slow steps and then, of course, he is here and, of course, we all sit here like my goldfish, all wide eyes and open mouth, and try to find a way to pretend we've been waiting for him all along.

In my father's hands, two small boxes neatly wrapped.

"Merry Christmas," he cheers.

"Merry Christmas," Mom and Jordan and my ginger aunt and her rabbit-faced daughter return. "And a Happy New Year," Jane adds a little too late.

Quickly, I don't think anyone else sees, my cousin looks to Jordan, and I understand what they were speaking about earlier. It was my cousin. She was always a special fan of my father's, her favorite (and only living) uncle. She let loose the lie and has been getting herself high all day to avoid the bad/good thing she's done.

My cousin takes him to the kitchen to grab a bowl and in those few short seconds we exchange more useless looks and stupid silence and when he returns, we resume a conversation we weren't having before he arrived.

"You look great," Jordan says, and I can see she means it, and he does. He's shaved and combed his hair and for once he wears a button-down and grease-free jeans.

I'm just beginning to think, to (in secret) thank the non-god for this course-correction, when Dahlia gets up. Sunny follows.

5. TIME LOST

DAHLIA leaves the table, the room, this floor. She goes to the basement, like all those before her, and Sunny follows. I'm pulsating. I am angry, I realize, an emotion I haven't felt in too long. Angry, I suppose, at the double-rudeness of my aunt, of Dahlia to respond to Dad's presence like this. He's come because he has a right to.

I am angrier, already, than I know I should be. I swallow the bite, all mushed together beans and pepper and onion and beef, that I have held in my mouth since Dad arrived. I stand and go in the path of my aunt and uncle down the long, carpeted stairs that announce my intentions. I find them not in the bathroom but tucked away in a guest bedroom my grandparents never use.

They are in the middle of their plotting when I approach, Sunny bending steeply to meet Dahlia's height. Their voices are low, quick. My goal is to confront them, but instead as their eyes home in on me, I freeze.

"We didn't know your dad was coming," Sunny says, returning to his usual, towering height.

"None of us did," I say.

"Someone did," Dahlia corrects, peering around me to see if any others have followed.

I wonder if they caught the look Jordan and my cousin exchanged, if they've pieced together who fucked up or, alternatively, who corrected our fuck-up. I don't say anything.

"We'll be back up in a moment," Dahlia encourages, squeezing my arm, the tractor-crushed one.

I don't say anything.

"Did you tell him?" Sunny asks me, sudden and quiet, like he's ready for the truth but already forgiven me.

I don't say anything.

"It's alright if you did," Dahlia says.

I want to answer, but I'm drowning. I take deep breaths and recover myself. My anger has waxed to embarrassment. For my father, for my cousin. Myself. I steel myself, so pliable, and finally, I can speak.

"Why don't you like him? My dad." I check behind me, try to measure my words. "I know he's been bad in the past, but he loves us. All of us."

Sunny and Dahlia both cast their eyes on the wall or the untouched guest bed which my grandmother has taken so much care to fix up. Then, they survey each other, both so very different, unlike siblings. Sunny leans down and I know what's coming. A lie.

Instead, Dahlia chimes in.

"It was a long time ago," she says, as if already making excuses for him. "But, well, you have to understand, your dad was pretty drunk." Her eyes, like a doe's, all care and caution. Prey. "He tried to say he thought I was your mom." She waves her hands to dispel the truth, which is too acrid for any of us to breathe. "It was just a kiss," she says, and Sunny places a hand on her shoulder like maybe that's an understatement, or maybe that it's good to get it out.

Dahlia opens her mouth to say more, but I stop her.

"It's alright. You don't have to explain." As if I haven't already asked her to open wounds.

She hugs me.

"But you're right, I shouldn't have been so dramatic about it. It's been a long time," and here is my aunt shrinking herself down for me and already I'm trying to apologize, to back track, but Jordan is on the stairs and calling my name and saying to come upstairs, and so I do, and I don't apologize, and I feel Dahlia's sweet perfume soaked into my skin when I re-enter the dining room and see the table cleared, all that good food, at least in my bowl, wasted, and Jordan and Dad are standing there, lone, holding the two boxes my father has brought.

He hands me one. Says he just wanted to give these to us and figured it'd be better to come here than show up at my mother's apartment. I think to say he could have called, could have done this and so many things differently, but I can see his eyes, like all the others, have passed from red to pink and his hands, like all the others, hold back a tremor, stuff down what can't be stomached.

I thank him and open the box and there in perfect lettering is my name carved into a pocket watch.

I think I hear him say something about making up for lost time, but my blood is roaring, and my ears are amplifiers and so all I hear and see and feel is one thing and I don't know how to name it and I don't know how to tell him, tell them, except by holding the thing tight and waiting for the flood to pass. Otherwise, I'll end up on the floor, black out, seize, and all that's happened or will happen tonight will pass in the shadow of my fragility. I look at him and in his mouth I see words, claims meant to soothe me, and promises meant to bolster me and remembrances meant to ground me. I know I need to say something, anything to show I love him, too.

Instead: Glug glug glug.

Nothing.

6. CONTRASTS

THE food is lidded into Tupperware for each of us, including my father, to take home. Half-a-dozen cinnamon rolls remain, and all are quick to offer one to me. No, I tell each of them. I've taken too much already.

I am surprised to find that a weight has lifted from the party. That even if he could have approached it better, most at the dinner are relieved that he came.

In the living room where the tall tree looms, my mother and father and cousin and aunt and my mother's siblings and my sister and my grandparents and I sit or stand or kneel on the carpet, pricking our knees with the tree's lost needles. Sunny and Dahlia have spoken to my father for the first time in years, and my mother, either because she found what she was looking for or realized the futility of her search, has taken to braiding my sister's hair and speaking to my father in a voice I rarely hear: conciliatory. Jane has sobered and, for once, my father is without the usual signs.

I learn that during my basement sleuthing, my grandmother asked, begged my father to stay. That, in Jordan's words, she's been spending her whole day secreting away her sobs until he showed.

None of us have anything to offer my father, but we make efforts.

With my new tools, I draw my family's portrait, all warm lines and cold shadows, because the trick is in contrasts. I offer it to him at the end, but he says no. He's taken too much. Best to keep it in safe hands.

Near midnight, we go our separate ways, not knowing yet the blessing this evening has provided us. How often we will, each of us, replay this night in the months and years to come. In bed, we gather our gifts around us, both too much and too little for what awaits us two weeks down the line.

Burn

The Brother

BURN

IT ends on a Saturday morning, hours before you're due for your sister's college volleyball match before either you or your mother shuffle out of your beds and greet the mildew and cigarette smoke layering your apartment. The doorbell comes to you first as a wren's warble in your dreams and then, when you wake, a threat. Neither you or your mother are the kind to answer the door, your sister's always the one to do it, and she is so far away from you now, so it rings and it rings until finally you're sitting on your mattress, heart booming, and your mother opens the door.

You've never heard a sound like the one she makes then.

IT begins with a fall. Onto the couch. Over the dog. Down the long nail-lined stairs of the farmhouse. Your father making sounds like you've never heard before. Small and closed in at the throat and then echoing throughout your young life. Your mother never catches him, never quiets his cries. It takes twelve years and a trip to rehab for her to pack you and your sister up, steal you from the country and force you to live in a rancid, cramped apartment she can't afford.

Seven years pass and all that time the bomb's wick burns.

IT ends with a lie. Your mother wailing for five minutes before she drags herself to your door and asks you to come to the living room. The presence of a police officer no longer surprises you. He doesn't look at you. He doesn't move from his spot by the door. When he leaves, your mother says she first assumed it was your sister dead that ushered this policeman to your door. That's why she screamed the way she did, she says. A lie.

You decide, the both of you, that your sister should play her volleyball game before you tell her, but she can't keep it in. She calls her friend and from the other line, you hear him make a sound you've heard a million times before. A gasp-sigh. An I'm-sorry-this-happened-but-we-both-knew-this-was-coming. Little consolation.

IT begins with a crash. Years ago. Of a four-wheeler into a bramble of thorny bushes. Into a ditch. It begins with your father coming home, stepping back into the farmhouse, blood carving a line from his ears to his collarbones, hands ghostly still, the skin of one eye, paper-thin, torn and resting on his cheek. The roundness of his eye you've never seen before. Your tears.

It begins with healing. But a body never free of injury.

IT begins with a whimper and ends with a bang. A last trip down the stairs. His head against the concrete, which has never been kind to any of you. As you watch your sister spike the ball, jump up, up, up, higher than you've ever seen before, you wonder if she already knows. Already, a weight has lifted from her body.

You tell yourself this was coming. You remember the times you'd hoped it would. Your sister, smacking high-fives all around as she scores the final point, has a look of triumph on her face. You hope that look can return after today. Next month. Next year. Time is a match and you, all of you, wicks to be burned.

III.
SURFACE

Clinton Lake

Another

CLINTON LAKE

EVERY time they got together it was like this. The sister would go back and visit the brother in their hometown, or the brother would come and see the sister in her college town. Almost always, it was the sister driving to meet the brother, because the former had more money and freedom than the latter, who was still in high school, still in community college, still in his dead-end central Kansas town instead of the sister's less-of-a-dead-end eastern Kansas town. The sister would buy lunch or dinner or take the brother to a movie, and they would avoid talk of their mother or their father, who was four years dead, or their grandparents, who they had taken too much from already and could take no more, for one or the other was sure to pass in the coming years. The sister wouldn't tell the brother about her latest depressive episode, nor would the brother mention his. The sister avoided talk of work, because her jobs were always revolving, always unsatisfying and underpaid. The brother would pretend, for those short days, that he and the sister occupied the same world.

When the sister knew the brother was nearly out of community college, that the fetters grounding him in their hometown were weakening, she invited him to her apartment for a weekend. She lived alone, and since her only cat had recently passed away she didn't mind the company of another beating heart. The brother hesitated, as he did toward any invitation from anyone to go anywhere, but he felt he had little choice but to accept. He had never learned how easy it could be to say no.

The brother recognized his mistake when he sat on the sister's beige litter-buried futon and noticed a lack of pillows and blankets set out. He spotted two rolls of sleeping bags, a collapsed tent, and cooking items barricading him from the door and knew the sister had misled him.

"Not again," he said, as if the sister would know what he meant. She did.

"Clinton Lake is much nicer than the mud heaps around Salina," she said, pulling a two-pound bag of beef jerky out of the cabinet and stuffing it into an overfilled grocery bag.

The sister knew her previous praises of the college town had done little to move the brother. Still, she suspected that his allegiances might change, that he might be willing to move out of their hometown, away from their mother and grandparents, from the legacy of death they had inherited from their father's fall, if she showed him the lake. If he dipped his toes into the water and felt the sun against his cheeks.

But the brother knew that the sister's sun was not his sun. Its rays didn't penetrate him as they did her, his skin so much darker than hers, scarred, and thicker than hers. And because it never absorbed into him like it did her, he was unmoved by the sun and its unbroken sky.

"Just for one night," she said, strapping on a backpack.

The brother knew that the sister wanted him to move there, to Lawrence, and still he came. He knew that among the supposed benefits—better jobs, more liberal politics—was another unspoken assumption on the sister's part. That the brother wouldn't be called anti-Asian slurs or asked to wear Chinaman hats at parties or harassed by women with fetishes or called anti-Mexican slurs, because people often mistook him for being Latino. In reality, the brother and sister were only a quarter-Korean, and while the sister inherited little from her mother's side of the family, the brother had black-brown hair and eyes and skin like the raw earth. He was first called a slur at age ten, when he and his two "actually Mexican" friends were playing hide-and-seek in a Walmart. The brother was reluctant to believe that this would change if he were to move from central Kansas to eastern Kansas.

The sister didn't make too many promises. This was a town of radicals, but also of soulless corporate-types ready to unhinge their jaws and swallow him whole. The brother would find more freelance work here, that was for sure, but he might also end up doomed to a call center, like she was.

"Are there ticks?" he asked as they set up the tent.

"Of course," the sister said.

"Shouldn't we, I don't know, spray ourselves?"

The sister said it was only for one night, and she had tweezers that could pry them out, easy. And didn't he remember burning ticks off their cats when they lived on the farm? That was another option.

"Lyme disease isn't something you mess with," the brother said.

"Lyme disease couldn't harm us if it tried. We are children of the soil, bred for bigger foes."

The brother never understood the sister's fixation on the country. Perhaps it was because he had spent three less years on the farm, being younger than the sister. Perhaps he didn't feel the way she did because the land he remembered was sickly. Terminal. Perhaps it was the land that didn't care for him as she claimed it did her. He was the one getting hurt all the time, accidents of parental negligence or pure bad luck. And if that were the case, screw the land. He had survived just fine in his middling Kansas town.

The brother choked down two cigarettes as the sister hammered down the stakes for the tent. It was May or June, one of the milder summer months. On the drive to a more secluded camping area, they had passed a school bus packed with children or college kids headed the same way. The lot itself had ten camping sites with built-in firepits, water taps, and bathrooms, but the sister was too anti-social for those spots. So, the sister parked in the lot, and they carried their supplies through the webbed trails and rocky creek beds until they found a five-acre spread of prairie grass looking down on the lake.

"Best to take the higher ground," the sister said, "to spy our enemies before they can approach."

"The only thing we need to worry about are ticks and snakes."

"And spiders," the sister said, as she noticed a palm-sized garden spider, all black and yellow and hovering a foot above their heads.

"Maybe we should move," the brother said.

"They're harmless," the sister said. "There was one on the side of the farmhouse, don't you remember?" The sister extended her finger toward the spider's abdomen. "It stayed there for hours and when Mom came up with a broom, it skirted down the wall and into the yard."

"Stop," the brother said, because the sister was halfway to touching the demonic thing. Of living on the farm, he remembered waking up to brown recluses and woodlouse spiders in his bed, on his chest. His sister had told him at a young age that everyone eats eight spiders a year while sleeping, but he knew the truth. They were collecting inside him, his insides all web and dead flies. Carved out. That was how he felt most of the time.

"Did you bring swimming trunks?" the sister asked, and the brother nodded, though he couldn't understand his sister's desire to visit the shore, given that she didn't swim anymore. "Then let's go down to the water."

"We don't have to."

"The water is clean and there are some nice spots to sit down."

"If you want to," he said, and she said she did.

A year before, the lake and surrounding counties had flooded. As they descended the hill, the trees blanched from the midriff down. The flood had washed away most of the beaches. All that remained were shelves of shriveled dirt, old channels where water had burrowed through. From there, the brother jumped in.

He felt his body expand, his limbs, feet, gut dissolve into the waters and become one of its many moving parts. It was cooling, but warm currents swept over him now and then and reminded him of summers, years ago, when he and the sister would run ice cubes over each other's arms. In the lake, he went under and kept his eyes open and found nothing, a void looking back. Nothing like the first lake he sank into, struck through with unnatural color. Roiling from something deep down, far away from them, in the lake's lowest well. Still, he couldn't remember who had spoken to him there or what it had said. Just the feeling. The low rumble. The movement before his sister grabbed his wrist and propelled them upward.

LATER, as the brother and sister wound through the trails surrounding the lake, they passed by a number of other campers. A mother and father carrying a young son, a girlfriend towing a boyfriend toward the water. The brother and sister came to the foot of two hills, one short and right up against the shore, the other tall and gradual, sloping toward the town, which was half a mile off from this side of the lake. They could hear the whirring engines of cars on the nearby highway.

The brother suggested the taller hill, given that he could see there were volleyball nets and playground equipment at the top. The sister suggested the shorter hill, because it gave a perfect view of the water and was just far enough from the marina that human contact was close to nil.

They made their way up the taller hill, and found the park teeming with sweaty, shirtless boys and nymph-like girls in bikinis, pulled straight from a movie. The sister begged the brother to turn back, but the brother insisted, until they were both swinging on a set meant for children, and some of the sweaty, shirtless boys were circling around them, asking if they wanted to play volleyball.

The brother told them that the sister had played college volleyball. She was sure to kick their asses.

"You don't look like brother and sister," one of the boys said, making a point of looking them over.

"Well, we are," the sister said, and the brother knew what she was thinking. That this was the most unoriginal observation that could be made about them. It was also inaccurate, their faces taking the same shape when they laughed or got angry.

The brother and sister followed the glistening boys toward the dump of sand, and the sister had first serve. They played boys vs. girls and in the first ten minutes the girls smoked the boys until their faces' shook red from embarrassment, from exertion. The brother, whose strength was exclusively in his lower body, couldn't serve up anything decent, and so the girls were victorious. They high-fived each other and shot up a middle finger at the boys.

At the end of the game, the brother walked back to the sister, and when the brother's back was turned from his teammates, one of the red-faced boys joked to the others, "Guess we should've played ping pong. Then maybe we'd of had a chance."

"What did you say?" the sister asked, because she wasn't what you'd call sheepish. She wasn't what you'd call a peacemaker. She was an instigator, the brother knew, in moments like this, and so the brother tried to pull the sister's attention away, but the brother was too late.

"Hey, Cherry Cheeks, what was that?"

The boys were all goofy grins and shrugged shoulders now.

"Nothing, it was nothing," the guilty boy said, but the sister wasn't stupid.

"You really see no other room for improvements? My little brother isn't your scapegoat."

One of the boys tried to tell the sister to ease up, and the sister hunched forward, ready to pounce.

"Ping pong. Why suggest ping pong? Not tennis? Not soccer? Not cricket or badminton or underwater basket-weaving?"

The unspoken answer was that Chinese people were all good at ping pong, or so white people liked to think.

And though the brother desired to stop her, he didn't, because he knew she would stew about it all night unless she got the fire out now.

"If I have to explain it to you, you've got something missing up there," the boy said, pointing at the sister's head.

The brother started walking off, because he knew it'd draw the sister away, and it did. The sister trailed behind him, still smoking, until she stopped. Curls of black left in her wake, she jogged back to the dump of sand where the boys remained joking and dripping with sweat.

"We're Korean you dumb fuck," she said, before kicking up a storm of sand and throwing armfuls at the all-red boy. It got in his eyes and his mouth and stuck to his sopping skin so that he became little more than a child's half-assed sand sculpture.

Then the sister ran off toward the lake and the brother followed and when they had put a safe distance between themselves and the boys, the brother hollered, and the sister yipped like a coyote, and it was the happiest they had felt together in years.

As they returned to their campsite, the sister spoke of the land here. The trees' chalky trunks reminded them that they were walking on claimed land, she said. If the waters claimed it once, they would claim it again. That is why she had suggested coming there. Who knew how long before the floods made the lake less and less accommodating.

The earth was not a forgiving mother, but a slow-burning, vindictive one, she insisted. The kind of mother who one minute suffocated her kids in adoration and beauty and slapped their wrists the next. And how had they, all their lot, treated their mother?

THE brother often wondered if the sister had properly graduated from Christian to atheist. Her delusions were never helpful ones.

And still, he preferred the water.

At their campsite, the brother and sister gathered sticks and lit a fire and shared ghost stories, but ones each had heard before, so that the danger and midnight anxiety were removed. They slept soundly inside their nylon home, and the brother ignored the spiders latching on to the outside of the tent, their bodies still, waiting.

"ONE more night. Why not?"

It was the brother's suggestion, and the sister agreed. No one would miss her, and their mother was unlikely to miss the brother, too.

As they trudged toward the lake once again, the sister thought about the dead body that had turned up inside a burning car shortly after the lake had ceased its flood.

THE brother dipped into the lake again, swam as deep as he could go. The sister hadn't told him about the burning body, or the young boy who had passed away in the waters less than a month ago. The sister didn't want the brother to think the lake was dangerous, given how much he had taken to it, and so she said nothing as he dove and resurfaced and swam farther and farther out.

The land had always protected her, and so it would protect him.

They passed few people that day. The winds had brought an unexpected chill, and for much of the morning and early afternoon, the clouds shut out the sun. The brother and sister walked miles and miles of trail leading low into valleys smothered with poison ivy, over rocky shores housing copperheads that, miraculously, didn't bite them, and far across uncut prairie grass where a tractor and rusted-out combine header sat, just waiting to give some untethered child tetanus.

The brother and sister ate a lunch of hash browns and eggs, cooked in their father's old cast-iron skillet, which the sister had taken from their mother's apartment when she moved to this college town. Given the way things were going, the sister decided on bringing up the topic of moving again.

"This town is more artists and musicians than anything else. We take care of our creatives here."

"Shouldn't I go somewhere with a scarcity of artists? You know, less competition?"

"You don't have to worry about competition. There are grants, fellowships, a full-fledged art museum." The closest art museum to their hometown was Wichita, over an hour away. "The art center is brilliant, and downtown Kansas City has a hundred galleries filled with middle-school level art. You'd outshine them."

The brother didn't like when the sister complimented him, because she always bent the truth. She overestimated him.

"The rent is almost double what it is in Salina," the brother said.

"And a third as much as any big city. Come on, you would love it here."

The brother decided to climb a nearby oak tree in order to end the conversation. He was fifteen feet up, swinging from a thick branch, when the sister begged him to come down.

"Stop," the sister said.

"Why?" the brother asked.

"Because it's dangerous."

The brother wanted to ask, was it dangerous because he might fall, or because the earth might retaliate for him being so callous, the tree's branch creaking from his weight. He didn't say anything. Instead, he pulled himself closer to the trunk and sat on a low-lying branch.

"What if I told you I didn't want to live anywhere?"

"What do you mean?"

The brother didn't answer at first, but he noticed the sister's face go hard. A curl of smoke wafted up to him, but it was lighter than shale. She wasn't angry. Just concerned.

"If you want to stay in Salina, I guess it isn't the end of the world."

"No, I mean, what if there's no place in the world for me?" Except the lake. Its bed so soft. Its company without demands.

But the sister wouldn't understand. She took his words literally.

"Why would you say that? You could make it anywhere. You haven't lived anywhere but Saline County."

"Okay," the brother said, but it wasn't the end of the issue for the sister. It flared up in her an alarm she hadn't felt in years. That the brother was in fact like her, like their mother, like their father. Prone to depressive states and, occasionally, contemplative of ending things sooner rather than later. The sister had had her own rough phase in college, and still it lingered in the very back of her skull, waiting for the most stunning days or promising relationships to wrap itself around her.

The sister didn't bring it up again. She didn't know how to help him, and she didn't know how to keep him safe from it. She hadn't kept him safe as a child; he was always getting hurt by their careless parents, racists, or some other kind of ignorant bullies at school. No matter whose eyes she kicked sand in, she couldn't stop him from being hurt.

But she didn't give up easily.

THAT night, they stirred up another campfire. The woods nearest them shattered the air with their multifarious voices: crickets, locusts, owls, coyotes, deer. The sister relished these noises, had once downloaded an app to her phone that would play a similar polyphony as she begged for sleep, but it hadn't been the same. The sister cooked up hamburgers and broke out a bag of Lays wavy chips, because the brother and sister were Kansans, and this was the most Kansas dinner of all. They ate quickly, scalding the roofs of their mouths.

They were quiet. The sister watched with faithful attention as the light dashed from the lake, the trees, the grass. The brother kept his eyes on the campfire, its cinders full of breath, living as much as he was.

When the time for sleep neared, the sister decided to make one last push, one bid to win his heart.

"If you were to move here, we could come down here as often as you want. From the north, it's just one turn out of town. It could be like when we were kids, kicking up dirt and swallowing muddy water."

The brother slipped a cigarette out and lit it. He took a few good puffs and blew the smoke toward the fire, so that its poison intermixed with the wood smoke.

"Is that what you remember?"

Their young lives had been one long, dramatic descent from life on the farm, from the peace that existed, or seemed to exist, in their youngest years. Before they learned how life lived on a farm was different from life lived in towns and cities. Flattened kittens and disappeared dogs, mange-ridden coyotes and the occasional mountain lion ready to push a reset button on everything around you. Blades of all kinds cutting, culling, whistling past you, and you, just a bag waiting to be pricked.

"This would be different. I could help you with whatever you need. A place to stay, finding work. I want you to know that things don't have to be how they've always been." Her life had changed, yes, when she had moved to this town, but was it better? Trading constant disorder for silence only shocked the system.

The sister kicked dirt onto the dying fire.

In the tent, they lay on their backs and opened up the screen looking up to the night sky. The town's glow blotted out most of the stars, but they took their time counting the ones pushing past the pollution.

For the first time in an hour, the sister spoke up.

"It doesn't matter. Live where you want to live. Just please, keep living."

The brother listened. Winced when he heard her voice break. He thought of cinders, where their heart must be. He had the desire to dig his hands in, crumble the ash until he found its bold, beating center. Instead, he watched a meteorite dissolve into the atmosphere.

"Fine."

THE sister lurched awake before the sun could arc above the trees. The smell of smoke stuck in her nostrils, and at first she wondered if the cloud had come from her, from some bad dream dropped from memory. Outside the tent, she watched a tower of tar-black clouds billow skyward. Their shape emanated from the direction of the lot she had parked in, half a mile off. Without seeing its source, the sister knew what burned there. Who had burned who.

She knew she should wake the brother, call the authorities, try to save whoever might be smoldering inside their soon-to-explode vehicle. Instead, she zipped shut the screens, shut them out from the outside world. She lay down beside the brother and pictured the earth's beating heart. Its breath her breath. She wanted to stir the brother, share with him this communion, but she knew this would only bring pain. That he would run for the car and, like her, witness the ineffable. That he would come back changed. And so she let the brother sleep and saved him this misery, if only for a few hours.

Rend, Sew

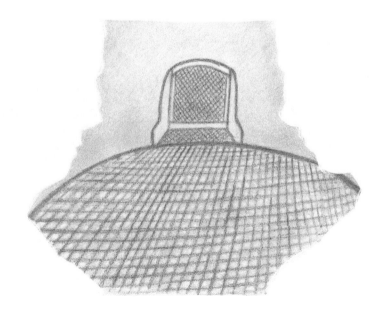

The Sister

REND, SEW

.

I GIVE you the best memory I have of my mother because there's competition for the worst.

It's the summer between third and fourth grade, so I'm nine years old. Chung is six. We're at the farm, where the good memories exist, and Mom has a plastic spyglass in hand. She's crouched and hopping around the yard littered with mewing kittens. Chung and I are fitted with small wraparound binoculars, black cylinders cross-eyed around our throats. We are in hot pursuit of a baby-bunny murderer, whose victim our mother has carefully hidden from our eyes. The cats, our prime suspects, are many in number. Thirty at least. Names I can hardly remember.

All of us, sweating and mud-whipped.

"A-ha!" our mother declares. "Footprints."

We scramble to her place in the lawn. She leans in close.

"Pawprints to be exact."

We groan in response. We know the culprit has paws. But who? Who massacred a defenseless little bunny?

Mom searches the grass before us, spyglass pushing her eyelashes skyward. Evidence, yes, but we have dozens of cats on the farm. We need something definitive to put the criminal in the clink. Kneeling beside her, my hands so cool in the mud, my naked face baking in the summer sun, I find it. Something definitive. Among the bits of fur, just-dried blood, and flattened grass where the murder victim had laid vulnerable before being dragged across half the yard and found on the porch—a faithful offering—I see a distinct set of prints. Two back paws. One front.

Hobbes. The three-legged cat.

Of course, I think. Of course it was him—the maimed, the abandoned, the isolated. Though I know his punishment will be non-existent, this children's game is just a distraction from whatever scream, whatever fight surfaced that morning or the day before or the week before, guilt sears my throat. I freeze up because I cannot name the guilty. I cannot charge one of our own.

When Chung sees the prints, he screams Hobbes' name. Our mother, satisfied, ruffles Chung's bowl-cut hair. She encourages us both. We celebrate the solved case with push-pops and a round of *Mario Kart,* and after I beg and beg to let the cats in, which we never do, she agrees. Thirty cats stampede. Our father won't be sober enough to notice the hundreds of muddy paw prints when he wakes from his nap.

IT hasn't been a year since she died. It is the day before Thanksgiving.

Our aunts, Jane and Dahlia, live here, in California, near Los Angeles with their adopted brother Sun. They have lived there together for over a decade. They haven't lived in Kansas, their homeland, our homeland, since their twenties. Chung and my flights were courtesy of our aunts. Our Uber ride is courtesy of our aunts. We are both in our twenties now, he mid-twenties, I late-twenties, so flights are out-of-budget. Travel in general is out-of-budget.

The Uber driver pulls up to our aunts' house, a peach stucco mini-mansion straight out of any boomer's dreams. Short palm trees cut the house into an idyllic triptych from our viewpoint. Our aunts' adopted brother, Sun, kneels before a hedge, clipping away.

"Thank you," Chung says to the driver, and I echo him.

"Thank you."

In the driveway, in the California dry heat, Chung and I call Sun by his nickname: Sunny.

He stands and wipes his forehead.

"Jordan, Chung. It's great to see you." He takes us in a big hug, but I am on the outskirts and a part of me is happy with it. Then our aunts are on the lawn, the two of them hugging us, too, and suddenly I am closer to the center than the edge and I only think of breaking free, this heat suffocating, this proximity uncomfortable.

Sunny takes our ratty duffel bags and sun-faded backpacks all at once.

Jane and Dahlia show each of us our rooms, modest in size but furnished with queen-sized pillow-top beds and TVs and unbelievably soft carpeting.

On the back porch of their mini-mansion, now late afternoon, Chung, Sunny, my two aunts, and I lounge on plush chairs and drink martinis by an amoebic pool.

Dahlia, at fifty-nine, is the youngest of the sisters. She was the closest to our mother, the one always getting her into trouble and, often, out of it. Jane, the oldest, was always on her own, as she puts it. She is the only sister to have been born in Korean War-time Tokyo. Dahlia and our mother were born after our grandmother was finally granted a visa, three years after the Korean War ended.

The arrival of Sun made little difference to Jane. She was already on her way out when he came into their home, having lived with his adopted family in Seoul until he hit eighteen.

Dahlia asks about Chung's freelance work. They ask about my schoolwork, the first semester of a graduate program in writing. Good. I tell them it's good. I don't tell them that I'm thinking of dropping out, that I don't find it worth the fifty grand it will end up costing me, only to waste ten years as an adjunct making starvation wages.

"Your mother would be so happy to see this," Dahlia says.

She's barely drunk her martini, but she's halfway to crying.

"She is happy to see this," Jane responds, the more Christian of the two. The more certain of our mother's salvation.

If our communal assumption about how she died is right (none of us have had the gall to follow up with the Police Department), and if Jane's religious affiliation is the right one, the real one, our mother is not in heaven. None of us talk about this. None of us talk about how I ended up with her ashes, bagged and stuffed into a small wooden box, a simple plaque with her picture, name, and birth/death dates on the front. How it sits on my bedroom dresser. How it shouldn't have ended up with me. A cruel joke, a poor decision on all our parts.

Dahlia looks straight into me, eyes wet. "Your mother was the kindest person." She sips her martini. "No one could say she wasn't kind."

I consider this argument for a moment. The implication of Dahlia staring at me as she makes this claim. I finish my drink and go inside.

In one of the four bathrooms, I dab my oily face—flying always draws it out of me. I work through the arguments in my head, arguments I will never verbalize. *Kind is one way to put it. She was kind when she called me a selfish bitch or a pathetic leech or urged me to kill myself during a depressive episode.*

And I don't linger on the things I said to her because, mostly, I can't remember them. I've never pretended I'm without blame for how things went, but Dahlia's words carve me and I have to breathe and sit and steady my hands.

When I've rallied myself, I go back outside.

When I come back out, I sit down by Chung. I wonder how he's feeling. If he's doing as good as he says he is. Two years have passed since he alluded to ideation or at least major depression.

"How's your martini?" I ask. I know that he, like me, didn't touch alcohol until he was well past twenty-one. This is the first time I've seen him drink.

He shrugs. "I feel," he struggles for a moment. "I feel liberated." He laughs. His cheeks have turned splotchy red. Dahlia's face is the same.

"Jordan, are you seeing anyone right now?" Jane pokes my arm.

I look to Chung. He anticipates my gaze and smiles to himself.

"No." There's a professor, long-haired and pencil-thin and ten years my senior, from my undergrad, not my grad program, who occasionally texts me and I occasionally meet at his office or at the park or in the swampy underbelly of the off-limits tunnels running under the school, but he's rarely single and I rarely find myself wanting to extend our time together past our stunted intimacy.

"What about you?" I ask Jane.

"There was this nice grocery boy," Dahlia says.

"He wasn't a boy," Jane responds. "He was thirty-nine. And we only went on one date. He preferred gin to vodka martinis, so that was that."

Jane is the only one, between herself, Dahlia, and Sunny, who have ever married. She's been divorced for ten years and dating guys half her age since, but they never stick.

No one asks Chung if he's seeing anyone. I know that he is. Rafael, who, in my modest opinion, is a bit of an ass. Chung always too ready to forgive.

Sunny brings up dinner and Jane and Dahlia debate for twenty minutes over the best restaurant in town. Then it's decided. We're headed beachside.

OUR maternal grandmother had a tumultuous life that started in Seoul and landed in Tokyo, before she met my grandfather, an American soldier fighting in the Korean War. She was thirty-four when they met. Thirty-five when they had their first child together, Jane, and forty when they married, finally, in the United States.

She had been abandoned too many times in her life. First by her mother, in death; second by her father when he remarried; abandoned by her brother who took her away to Tokyo and let his wife abuse her; abandoned by the Japanese man she was mistress to. She, in her adulthood, became willingly or unwillingly a comfort woman. Spent years tethered to Japanese Imperial Army bases. When she eventually became pregnant and was, again, discarded, she decided to have her child in Seoul. She sewed money into her undergarments and pretended she was visiting her husband in Korea.

Our grandmother boarded a ship too late into her pregnancy. Slowed by tremulous storms, the boat didn't make it to Seoul. They had to turn back, wait out the weather. She gave birth to (who we can only assume to be) Sun on a ship, storm-soaked. Homeless. This is how Sun came into the world.

She did make it to Seoul, eventually. For a year, she raised him, but after he caught and nearly died of a fever, our grandmother saw little choice but to adopt him away to a wealthier family.

Seventeen years later, Sun showed up, no explanation, straight from Seoul he said, claiming to be our grandmother's son. Our mother's half-brother. He, according to my mother, didn't look like he'd come straight from Seoul. He was skeletal, skin so dark he must have spent his days outside (and the darkness of a Korean's skin was always tied to class, to work, my mother would say because her mother would say). His shoes were coming apart at the toes and heel. He looked like he could have walked cross-country, not flown cross-continents, so my mother never trusted him. Then again, she didn't trust most people.

$\bigcirc$.

AT dinner, Chung and I gorge ourselves on more kindness. Blackened shrimp, risotto, fried oysters. Sun sits between us, an unintentional disruption, I'm sure, but it makes me uneasy. I drink two glasses of red wine, which can't be cheap, but it quells my anxiety.

After, we sit on the beach, chase swift spotted crabs, and gather shards of seashells to propel back into the ocean.

Dahlia blazes a joint and we all take a few hits.

Toward twilight, Chung, Dahlia, and I wander down the beach.

"You know your mom always wanted to see the ocean."

We never visited our aunts when our mother was alive. We couldn't afford it, and our mother never wanted to borrow money until she was desperate, which she often was, but never for the right reasons. Dahlia and Jane always came to Kansas to visit. I had only seen Sun twice before this trip.

I want to tell Dahlia to stop, to give us just a little more time, a little more freedom to forget. I can already tell she will cry if we continue, and I can't handle the crying.

"Yeah," I say. "She bought beach-themed calendars every year."

Dahlia, Chung, and I have walked two miles at least. The stars would be out, but the light pollution chokes them.

"Should we head back?" I ask. Dahlia has started to limp, a bad hip, and I know she won't turn back until we suggest it.

"Yeah, alright," she says.

Chung is barefoot, toes caked in gold-gray silt. He throws his shoes at me, half-drunk. He had a second martini at dinner and his face is crimson. "No! I want to go swimming." Suddenly, he runs into the ocean, shorts sprayed with saltwater kicked up from his splashing, arms waving. His black-brown hair scatters in the wind. His gold back is just tinted pink from too much sun. Our mother always told him he didn't need sunblock because of the darkness of his skin, and that, unlike my translucent skin, his couldn't burn. All the time I worry her poor guidance will doom him twenty or thirty years down the line. Always, I inspect his arms and neck and back for signs of malignance when he isn't looking. He runs parallel to the beach, but ever deeper, away from us, jumping over shallow waves.

Dahlia is quiet a moment. I can hear her sniffing, the muscles in her throat swallowing, tight. I think of putting an arm around her, but I can't bring myself to do it. Then, she touches my arm and I know what's coming.

"I really miss your mom," she whispers, just for me to hear.

Chung is slowing pace, half-drenched, breathless.

A few stars near the horizon pucker up.

"I really think she got a bad deal, you know. She was too kind for—," she stops short.

I'm inching away from her hand, and I feel that I'm sinking.

"Please stop saying that," I ask. I walk off, back toward Sun and Jane.

THE first time I meet Sun I have just turned fourteen. Chung is eleven. Our parents have split at this point. Our mother has ushered us out of the farm, and we live in a two-bedroom apartment, our mother sleeping on the couch. Dahlia, Jane, and Sun fly out from California for our mother's birthday. Our mother doesn't have many friends anymore, and the friends she does have are always selling her oxycodone or meth or promises of a better life they never intend to deliver. So, our mother would have spent her birthday alone with us if her siblings didn't fly down.

Sun is the last to enter our apartment, wrapped in a too-large, fake-fur-lined coat close to his face. I have only seen him in pictures as a young man. In his fifties, he is and isn't the man I expect. Reserved, delighted and sprung with light at the sight of Chung and me. He hugs us so hard.

"You two look just like your grandma," he says, and he emphasizes this point with me. "Those cheeks! Just like hers." I have been told this before. I look remarkably like her, only with translucent skin and freckles and green-brown eyes. Usually, this warms me. I ache to know my grandmother, who died a year before I was born.

"Chung, your aunts said you like baseball. You want to throw the ball around in the parking lot?" This is an odd request, given that it is bone-chilling cold and snowing outside. November in Kansas.

Before Chung can answer, and he would have answered yes, our mother cuts in. She leans forward, claps one hand against her back, the other hand on her hip, "Jump on," she commands, wide stanced, sensai-style. Chung laughs and complies. Suddenly strong again, for the moment, she carries him piggy-back away and makes crazy circles. The world teeters, Sun backs off and accepts a mug of hot cocoa from Dahlia, who has taken to microwaving a mug for each of us, marshmallows and all. In our half-living room, we crowd on the couch and tacky carpet. Finally, Chung is dumped on our laps. We've never had so many people over at once before.

Dahlia directs her voice at our mother. "How's the airport going?"

Our mother picks cigarette ash out of her hair. "I quit that place two months ago. The manager was an ass," she says, and Dahlia looks nervously at us, as though we'll crumble at the mention of the word.

"I'm sorry to hear that."

Jane asks if she can't get something special for her hot cocoa (vodka) and our mother's skin flares. She stopped drinking years ago, due to our father's problem.

Sun stays silent during most of this. When conversation stills, he speaks up.

"We brought a few small things," he says, "but we sent a few packages in the mail, too. Should arrive in a few days."

"Happy birthday!" Dahlia says, face lighting up. She hasn't seen our mother in at least two years and is particularly emphatic about the celebrations.

"You didn't have to do that," our mother says, though no one believes her.

Sun pulls out a small box from his coat pocket. Dahlia picks up two she clearly wrapped, precise, straight lines. Our mother tears them open. She laughs and screams at Dahlia and Jane's gifts: a lightweight leather coat and DVD set of *The Fellowship of the Ring*, which our mother adores. When she comes to Sun's gift, she makes an effort to stiffen her face. She doesn't look at him. Inside the small, thin box: a silver locket decorated on the outside with daffodils, her favorite; inside the locket, a faded photo of our grandmother pressed into one side.

Our mother hops up and hugs Jane and Dahlia. She thanks them. She doesn't say a thing to Sun, and my stomach boils, my face flushes in embarrassment.

We go to Gutierrez's for dinner, a local Mexican restaurant that has the best flour tortilla chips. Our aunts and Sunny refrain from alcohol on our mother's behalf. We indulge in every way—mountains of queso, beef-topped nachos, sodas and desserts all around. We never get to eat out. Our mother never gets to be celebrated in this way, not once in my memory. When it comes time to settle up, Dahlia, Jane, and Sunny split the bill.

In the car, our mother donning her new coat but not her new necklace, she leans against Dahlia and says how happy she is.

At the apartment, we watch *The Fellowship of the Ring*, and Jane and our mother recite every line with precision.

"Pause it," our mother says. "Who needs a smoke break?" Both of our aunts go outside, and Chung insists on going too, because he wants to catch the snow on his tongue. Suddenly, Sun and I are alone. He took the floor during the movie. I ask him, wouldn't he want the couch? He's an old man, he deserves it.

"I'm not that old," he says, though he groans as he stands up from the carpet. "You, on the other hand, are ancient," he says to me. I laugh. I have been brought up to mistrust this man, but this is not the changeling I have been told of. He is jovial, kind.

"The locket is really beautiful," I tell him.

"Thank you," he says, spying its splayed-open box on the floor.

"Do you miss Grandma?"

He blinks a half-dozen times. "I do. I wish I had gotten to spend more time with her. She was a great woman." He must sense my interest because he continues, "Your mom is a lot like her." This I can't believe. I want her to be kinder, more trustworthy. "She was a fiery woman," he says. "I mean that in a good way."

When everyone returns, our mother pulls me into my bedroom. Her hair is dusted with snow and wind-swept. Her eyes bridge on wild.

"Don't listen to what that man tells you, Jordan. He's not who he says he is."

She's grabbed my arm; she twists, intentionally or not. She must have seen that we were having good conversation when she came in.

"He seems fine to me," I say, shaking her off. "He's nice."

"Don't be stupid," she whispers, as if he is in the room. Now she takes my wrist and squeezes. "He's an imposter. Don't listen to me. Fine. But he's not who he says he is."

When I return to the couch, when I sit next to Sun, I spy a reservation in his face. He analyzes me from the corner of his eyes. He knows. I don't know if it is this secret observation, or his change in demeanor over the rest of the short trip, but something in me holds onto what my mother said. I already don't care to trust people. I don't want to be duped.

The next time our aunts and Sunny visit, a few years later, this time for Christmas, Sun keeps his distance, as if he understands that he and I will never have the kind of relationship he had hoped for.

THANKSGIVING dinner is Thanksgiving dinner. Turkey, gravy, potatoes, niceties.

What are you thankful for, Dahlia?
For our wonderful family, each of us together, happy.
What are you thankful for, Jane?
For the loving presence of God, our salvation.
Sun?
For my kind sisters, my beautiful niece and nephew. For peace.
Chung?
For our health.
Jordan?
For our survival.

THE day after Thanksgiving, the day before we head back to Kansas, Chung and I spend the morning with Sunny.

We wander the streets, too packed and littered with trash, and lick ice cream off our fingers and buy postcards from a guy on roller-skates. Around noon, Chung spots a tiki-themed bar and insists we go.

"Two piña coladas, please," Chung orders, "and a Coca-Cola for my uncle." He smiles at Sunny, who nods at him. DD's don't drink.

Sunny picks a table on the patio. The metal table and chairs are hot from the sun, but I don't suggest moving. Chung sits across from me and Sunny next to me. I feel my muscles twitching, uncomfortable.

Chung's already a third through his drink before I've started mine.

"So, Sunny, where did you live before you came here? I mean to the U.S." Chung asks. Chung longs to learn more of Korea, plans on visiting there someday when he has money. If he has money.

Maybe it is Sunny's meekness, his seeming happiness, that makes me question him, that makes me think, even to this day, that's he played a joke on all of us. I distrust happy people. I need to force them to show their unhappiness, to stop their lying.

Sunny sighs, twists his coke bottle on the table.

"It was a long time ago," he says. "It doesn't feel like my life anymore."

My mother's voice in my head: maybe because it wasn't.

"I used to think I made the wrong choice coming here," Sunny says, avoiding eye contact. "Your grandmother, you know, never expected to see me again. She had sold me to a childless couple in Seoul who gave her money to—" and he stops. "To quit doing her job."

"We're not kids," I remind him. "She kept soldiers company. We know."

"Well, she met your grandfather not long after, so it didn't matter much. He sent her money when he had to go back to the U.S."

"But what happened before you came here? If you lived with a nice couple in Seoul, why leave? Why fuck up your mother's family by coming?"

The words are out of my mouth before I can field them. My mother coming through, I think. But no, it's just me.

I see the hurt in Sunny's eyes. The faint discoloration growing in his cheeks. He's sinking into himself. Chung is staring at me, his face red-splotched and his smile gone.

I form an apology in my mind, repeat it over and over, but I can't get it out.

When my brain fails me, I walk inside the bar, go to the bathroom, and slap myself on the cheek.

"Stop," I tell myself. Stop being a bitch. Stop being your mother.

When I go back outside, I see Chung and Sunny sitting across from each other, both silent, both bowed slightly forward. They could be the same person, four decades apart, I realize. The same wide, upturned noses, the same round cheekbones, the same outward-poking ears. I've never seen them in this way before. I feel like crying, for how stupid I've been. To buy into my mother's conspiracy.

"Hey," I say as I sit down, but before I can recite my apology, Sun stands up and heads out of the patio, onto the street.

Chung doesn't look at me. "He said he needed to get something from his car."

I nod my head, sip at my melting drink. The tiny paper umbrella twirls back and forth in the wind.

"Why would you say that?" Chung finally asks.

I pause. Take two anxious breaths.

"I don't know. It was dumb. I just remember Mom saying—,"

Chung interrupts me. "Mom? Mom was so mean to him. She bullied him the whole time they lived together."

"What?" I stare at him, confused. "How do you know that?" Chung has never talked to me about our mother's cruelty. He would always sit silent in his room when she and I would fight. Even when she would try to pull him in, try to make him a part of it, he never said anything.

"She always talked about how he screwed up their family. Grandpa was so furious that Grandma hadn't told him she'd had a son. That she would sell him off."

"That's why I said—,"

"And because of that, Mom tormented him every day. You remember her talking about burning his GED books? How she told all her friends he was a creep so no one would talk to him?"

And then I remember. Our mother had a knack for bragging about the worst things. About beating up a girl in middle school for calling her a gook. About dragging a boy by the hair when he didn't ask her to homecoming. She had bragged about lying to her friends about Sunny. About making her dad believe Sunny was drinking his beers when he was at work.

"I just, I didn't think about it that way," I say. My face is scorching. "I'm sorry," I say, but I can see Chung wants to move on. Sunny is gone for some time, and Chung and I finish our drinks without a word. I offer to buy him another drink, but he declines. I can see he's thinking through something, his eyebrows brought together, his lips quivering to mirror the words in his mind.

Just as Sunny comes into view, halfway down the block, Chung speaks up.

"Why would you assume he had a nice family? When he was a kid. When he was in Seoul."

I don't know what to say.

Sunny returns with a small, wrapped gift. He wanted to give it to us when Jane and Dahlia weren't around, he says. He doesn't get to see us often. He just wanted to give it to us.

Inside the wrapping: a tattered book in Korean.

"I only have one, but maybe you can share it," he says. He had handed it to me, but in my guilt, I let Chung hold it. "It's a Korean to English dictionary. You can read it both ways. I thought maybe you might want to learn someday."

I meet Sunny's eyes for the first time since he's come back. I take both his hands in mine, his hands so coarse, dry, hot. "Thank you," I say, but I know it's not enough.

OUR mother's memorial service was held at a different mortuary than our father's was. This only made the differences in their services more apparent. My father—who over his fifty-something years had been a farmer, a builder, a contractor, a Tae Kwon Do instructor—saw over three hundred friends, family, and students attend his funeral. There was no standing room left when the service began. Our paternal grandparents were there, all our first and second cousins, distant great-uncles, great-aunts. My classmates and their parents.

At my mother's service: Chung, myself, my aunts, two past Tae Kwon Do students, and my mother's Tae Kwon Do instructor, a South Korean man of seventy-five who was a twelfth-degree black belt, who had once served in the ROK Army. There was a brief prayer. A shoddily edited video compiled what few photos we had left after Chung, my mother, and I had left the farm mid-summer. At the end, they played *Turn, Turn, Turn*, one of her favorite songs. The CD began to skip halfway through, so we switched it off and tried to play it off one of our phones. It wasn't the same.

Sunny didn't go to our mother's service. He was too unwell to make the flight. At least that's what Dahlia told us.

THAT last night after Thanksgiving, we convene around a fake fireplace in the peach-stucco mini-mansion's smaller living room (there are two). The lights are dimmed, and Jane plays fifties jazz like our grandfather liked. Sunny makes us all martinis, Chung a dirty martini, because he has discovered he loves them. Dahlia spent her career as a pianist, so later, when we are tired of jazz, she plays Beethoven's *Moonlight Sonata* on the grand piano.

We become shadows in this light, shaped by the LED flames. The night is cool so we open the windows, the patio door.

Chung tries his hand at the piano when Dahlia has tired. He's not half-bad. His body becomes fluid, rolling and tilting and shrinking as an improvised melody springs into the room. He has always been the more artistic of the two of us. His music haunts, deep tones with discordant, slow melodies overlaid. Sudden bursts of energy, movement.

Just as Chung finishes one piece, I see Sunny go outside onto the back porch. I look around the room, see if anyone will notice my departure. Jane and Dahlia are too absorbed, rightfully, in Chung's music, so I slouch into the outdoors.

I find Sunny sitting in front of the amoebic pool, which twists lines of blue light over his figure as the water jives below him.

"Sunny," I say. I touch my hand to his shoulder, careful not to be too firm.

He has never said it, but I know he feels the same discomfort about physical affection that I do. He's slouched just a few inches forward, as he's always been, but he suddenly straightens up, trying to appear larger. Predators about.

I sit down by his side, not too close, and cup my hands into the pool water, entranced.

"Sun, I'm sorry. I really am sorry. And it's not just that I shouldn't have said that thing earlier about your other family," I continue. "I shouldn't have believed it."

He stays silent, but he sits down next to me. He dips his fingers just into the pool.

"You belong in *our* family and I'm happy to know you," I say. For the first time, I mean it. He sees this, I know he sees this.

"Thank you," he whispers, hard to hear above the lapping of the pool. "I know it's been hard for you," he says. "It's not easy." He wipes at his nose. "People die and you lose the time to make things right."

I think of telling him to stop because I can feel the floodgates malfunctioning. I swallow.

"There are lots of things I wish I told your grandma, you know. Took too long, thought we'd have time to talk." I feel the feather weight of his hand on my shoulder, so hesitant it almost hovers in the air. "Time for me to say what I thought I needed to say. About her leaving me. About being erased. But you can't linger on it. You have to find your own way of making peace with it."

Before I can staunch it, tears salt my cheeks and collect in my shaking hands.

"It's okay. You'll be okay," he says.

I hadn't seen or talked to our mother for seven months before she died. Chung was the one to find her. To come back to her apartment and find she'd been dead for three days. That she'd probably swallowed all of the pills she had. That she'd had thousands of dollars in suddenly accrued debt, skyscraper-high interest rates. That she'd gotten a DUI weeks before, for driving under the influence of her medications. He was the one to walk into this, to have to grapple with it head-on. I haven't had that certainty. The idea that she is dead still can't solidify in my mind, because I never saw her body, only the box that holds her ashes and stares at me every night as I can't sleep, as I dream of water walling up and nothing else.

When I've tired myself out, we head back inside. I don't try to hide my wet face or red eyes. Chung plays a lament.

IT'S past midnight, probably three or four. We've been up so long Jane has passed out in an armchair. Chung has given the piano up and we're all, conscious or not, circled around the faux-fire. Dahlia has pulled out a photo album and she, Chung, Sun, and I look over the firelit pictures. Much of them are black-and-white, faded, yellowed with time. A few of them poke out from their plastic casings, and I finger the edges, leaning over Dahlia's shoulder.

Photos of our mother's family, before Sun. At the trailer park where they spent their youth. Clotheslines swaying in the distance, our grandmother, both hands planted on her hips, a wide grin punching up her cheeks. A face like and unlike my own. Photos of the family with Sun, where, truly thin, he looms behind the group smiling, but less so than everyone else. Another photo: our mother, Dahlia, Jane, and Sun all together. They're all gripping one another's sides, shoulders, all teenagers but some closer to adulthood. Our mother is half-jumping in the picture, her hair sent skyward, her teeth reflecting light back at the camera. This is what I want to remember of her, but I know that isn't possible. That it's from another life.

"I don't want to go back home," Chung says, touching the photo. "I want to stay here."

I nod my head, press my fingers into the exposed photograph edges. It feels unbearable, going back to school, to work, to a world so much lonelier than this one.

"You know," Dahlia says. "Your mom told me she had the best Christmas, this last year." She looks at me, and for the first time I don't redirect. She hugs my side and points to a photo of our mother and grandmother.

I don't know, but this conversation steers me to an idea. One I haven't conjured in too many years.

"Let's go," I whisper to the others. "I know it's late."

Chung, Sun, and Dahlia look up at me. They're ready for whatever I have in mind.

THE ocean is black-cold. Temperamental, though the weather has been calm. Still, we let it wrap around our ankles. Chung and I have changed into swimsuits. The sun is distant, below the horizon, but its light is just reaching us, just pulling us up.

This is our last chance, our last chance to be together, to *live* together, as one, before the trip is over and Chung and I go back home and who knows when we will see us all together again, if we will see each other again at all.

Dahlia has her phone up. She takes poorly lit photos of Chung and I splashing gleeful in the low water. She takes a picture of Sun off to the side, and Jane lying on the beach half-asleep but unwilling to miss this.

Chung and I grasp hands, wade a little longer, a little deeper. The wind whips us, and the water is cold, but his hand is warming, assuring. A part of me knows, a part of all of us knows, this is where we'll take her. This is where we'll release her when the time is right.

I am struck with the desire to go farther, to give ourselves a little more to dip into, to work against. First, Chung and I go waist-deep, armpit-deep. As the waves swallow my shoulders and my feet release the sand, my heart quickens, blood rushing, but I stay there. Let go Chung's hand and in his eyes I see his relief. I take all the air my lungs can hold, brace myself, and sink. I discover all the colors I've robbed myself of, the swell and give of the water I've missed. I stay there as long as I can hold it, and when I return, the world is breached anew.

Grandma Kim at 45: a serigraph

The Brother

GRANDMA KIM AT FORTY-FIVE: A SERIGRAPH IN FOUR LAYERS

1/10

GRANDMA Kim had a rose-petal mouth. See the ballooned lips, half-inch creases trapping her mouth at each end. Such shapes are difficult to translate in their three-dimensional splendor on paper. She smiles, but a printed smile is not a living smile. I would like to have seen her grin for myself, but then again, art is the playground for reanimating the dead.

2/10

GRANDMA Kim curled her hair, her pretty black hair, our mother would say, showing us the formless crimps of her own broken and burned hair. What a mistake. Our grandma's hair could be like ivy when left to its good nature: voracious. Here she has pinned it down, her bangs the only moving part, and they too show little of her unmuted self.

3/10

THIS print is of my grandmother, whom I never knew, and so it is of my mother and my sister and myself, too. You cannot see her large front teeth or the slight bowing of her calves or the delicate arc of her nose, but I tell you they are there and in my mother and my sister and me too. Her body divided into my mother divided into my sister and me.

4/10

SCREEN printing demands that you separate the world into discrete layers, but so too does it force you to see the glory made in overlapping them. Blue ink overlays gold and soars into a fertile green so that my grandmother's garden pops, as it must have then, so much care given to the nurturing of things. See that birth. Note the flush of her tomato vines. Observe the hard lines that separate my grandmother's hair, her body, from the background. No such lines exist in this world.

5/10

EACH layer: run a test, note the placement with tape, pull fast and with strength and without breathing. Too slow, this layer, the gold of my grandma's skin, which also blends with the plush blue of my grandma's sky to create the green foliage. The paper has stuck to the screen and now my grandma's unblemished skin and her garden are pocked and bubbled, the ink left reaching toward you. This, too, is natural.

6/10

PLACES can be haunted, we are told, but people must be haunted, too. My mother always spoke of incidents in her adulthood, before I or my sister came. Of a crushing feeling over her legs as she slept. Of sounds and voices that had no physical birth. She always believed her apartments to be occupied. She never considered that it was her bones, her blood that sabotaged her. Her hauntings stopped only because my grandmother channeled herself into me before birth. See the doubling of the linework, impossible without running the ink twice, and I tell you, you see in those twinned grandmothers her ghost making herself known. She deserves to be known.

7/10

GRANDMA Kim wore an apron even when she walked my mother and her sisters to school. Even when she went to the movies. The only time she ever untied its strings, our mother would say, is when she would go to church with my mother and her sisters or when she would lay with her husband, who neither attended church nor went to the movies, so that he only ever saw her hips free when they made love. Note the fraying here, the delicate wash from a clean cream to the gritty brown marking years of use. We call this a rainbow pull, the melding of two colors in one layer. Some rainbows are not vibrant. Some rainbows are dishwater.

8/10

SEE the fumbling of the sky, the ink that just kissed the surface of the paper, leaving so much desire in its wake. My mother would say that our grandmother was a perfectionist, every garment sewn in rigid lines. No errant threads. You might call me a bad grandson for presenting the unruly and off-kilter versions of this print but let me remind you that to honor your ancestors you must build on their triumphs. A seamless garment. A seams-bared serigraph.

9/10

YOU might say this was not the assignment. You might say that you asked for ten matching prints, and I tell you that these are the same. Identical in their sloppiness, their mishaps. No more perfect symmetry exists than in the misguided, the malformed, the tainted.

10/10

GRANDMA Kim was born in Seoul and died in Kansas, not even seventy, not even a grandmother yet. A hard life takes its toll in hidden ways and yet, my grandmother kept going, even in death, to know my mother, to know me. She spent her years escaping to Tokyo, escaping to my grandfather's barracks, escaping to his American home with its American layers, so opaque, so unreadable. See her spirit in these eyes. See her reading you and everyone else, finally, with the clarity of the unbounded.

Endings

The Sister

ENDINGS

ONE burning sun and a system of less-luminous planets, orbiting, orbiting, occupy the living room when I arrive. June, so vibrant, so round, bursts at the seams with baby Rey, who is due to show her face in the coming weeks. These women, June's friends, circle her dressed in navy and bold hues, trying their best to be celestial, and here I am, dressed in black like the near-vacuum of space, like I'm expecting a funeral instead of a baby shower, and maybe I am.

Thirteen years exist between the last time I saw June and today. Thirteen years since the star of our original system, Amy, supernovaed herself and left us drifting and untethered. According to her email, Amy is coming, too, but standing in June's living room, I see only unfamiliar faces. Baby showers are for the falsely hopeful, and already I regret driving the two hours from Lawrence to Salina to attend. The sky shot down freezing rain and snow squalls all the way here, and my return won't be easy.

"Jordan." June's solar-flare arms reach for me. "I'm so glad you could make it. We were just about to open the champagne."

June's pregnant-woman hands, hydrogen-bright, push me into the orbital of guests. One passes June the champagne, who positions the bottle's bottom on her belly. With bruising force, the cork pops and baby Rey feels for the first time, I think, the jolt of our collective births—the BANG before our scattering, our furious rush to push out, away, until our shared origins are distant memory. The women around me laugh and cheer, and one of them hands me a glass bubbling over. June drinks diet coke and sits, knees tucked under, in the middle of us. Her stomach overarches and flattens the carpet below, and I wonder how at such an angle she can keep from toppling forward.

The sleet The cold. I begin to doubt that Amy will show. She was never one to burden herself to serve others, and she always hated driving on days like this.

I didn't believe her email when I saw it, three weeks ago, when June's baby shower email had gone out. Her reply had been short—

Be there, J.

—which might have been simple enough if our names were not June and Jordan. If Amy had just been clearer. I wasted hours poring over those words. *June, I'll be there.* or *Jordan, be there*—either way the comma was wrong. Whether it was meant as a confirmation or a command, I decided to reply, to come here, because I have waited thirteen years for this moment, to get answers out of her that she will never give up on her own.

That last day, our last day together, two months after our high school graduation, etched into me like muscle memory, our movements ebbing still in my blood. I've run it over and over again and still never decided on Amy's truth or dishonesty. The gust-whipped prairie. Vodka dimpling over Amy's lips. My shorts that didn't want to fit after. Amy's fingers, struck through by the sun, left bunny-ear shadows on my stomach as she claimed we were made for each other. That's why she had to leave, she said. A harmony as perfect as ours was damned. Putting as much distance between us was our only salvation.

Stunned at first, my rage came slow, preceded by confusion, and with it my smoke, which always gives away my emotions before I've decided on naming them. A thick umber cloud billowed, bigger than I'd ever released before. Amy tried to calm me; I tried to seal my lips and nose shut, but the thing proved untamable. Amy had to step back, let me wear myself out before we could talk again. My rage flowed because I knew Amy lied. She wasn't trying to save us. She was a coward. For the first time in our six-year friendship she was letting fear rule her. Fear of commitment, her distaste of sweetness (whenever we kissed, she pinched my arm, my stomach, the meaty ingress between my thumb and forefinger) doomed us.

And still . . .

I tried to convince her to stay.

I DROWN my anger in champagne lest the smoke return now and ruin
June's shower, because after all these years, I still haven't been able to quiet
the little fire inside me. I watch June gather our gifts around her, and in her
hypnotic light I cool down.

Even after twelve years, June's face is nearly the same—big cheeks,
plum-sized chin, wideset baby-blue eyes that pierce right to your molten
core. Her hair had always hung in half-tidied pigtails. Now she's cut it at
the jaw and lets it hang in its tangled glory.

Hot, deep-in-the-stomach love pounds in me as I watch June finger our
many gifts, eyes glittering with hope, because I think she's relying on this
afternoon to settle questions for her, too. Her emails, the few words she's
spoken since I've gotten here, she's laced them all: *will I be a good mother;
will my daughter love me; will my husband love me; what are the ways I
can fuck this up and please can you help me avoid them?*

How stupid I was, I think, to leave this friend behind a dozen years
ago. Doubling our loss. And now I've come at the end of things. That June
invited me, that she remembered me at all, warms me from the near-blizzard
outside. I decide to scoot onto the carpet and hug her and tell her how sorry
I am but before I do— two beams of light cut into the livingroom through
the picture window. A car approaches, silent in the way only the rich are
allowed to be. At first I assume it to be Mr. Albright, June's husband, whose
face has yet to be seen and who, I've gathered through the baby-shower email
chain, is not particularly welcoming or attentive or fond of celebrations like
this one. I say I've come at the end of things not because motherhood is
equivalent to death. Fuck anyone who says so. I've come at the end because,
though I've never met him, I know men like Mr. Albright, have slept with
or gotten close with men like Mr. Albright, and from the little I have heard
of him, I can say June is headed down a road with only one exit. She's too
kind to forge other routes.

The car door opens, but it isn't him.

Amy, cast white against the snow, our sun, the real one, piercing
through, steps out of the passenger-side door. Amy, with her peat-black
hair wrangled into a ponytail, with her lips painted red and her Scarlett

Johansson proportions obscured by a royal-blue jumpsuit with bone-white stripes, arrives in the passenger seat of a rich person's car. In the ten steps between the curb and June's front door, she sucks down a cigarette.

June sits comfortably on the floor, surrounded by paper-wrapped promises of an easy birth and easy mothering, and so she asks for someone to open the door for Amy. For a moment I think it's going to be me—all my unanswered questions and unfettered anger neutralized in that singular greeting—that our reunion will be this simple, that quick. Before this fantasy fully materializes in my brain, one of June's friends opens the door.

Amy levitates into the living room, no more than an apparition of her teenage self, because there is so much foreign in this Amy, who has apparently lived a life of luxury. The real Amy, like me, like June, had grown up in the dirty, bloody country and learned of lack in her early stages. This Amy is not our Amy, and I wonder for one liberated moment if that means we are no longer hers, too. With one glance, with one motion, I see that isn't true.

Amy declines a chair by the kitchen and instead kneels by my armchair. She has yet to look at me straight, and still she turns down a glass of champagne, angles her arm back and says in her unchanged voice, "Jordan and I can share."

I hand her my glass.

June picks apart our gifts one at a time: a mountain of planet-printed onesies, a solar-system mobile, and rocket-decorated shoes impossibly small. I have given June a set of cartoonish astronaut decals to decorate the nursery, because she and Mr. Albright are apparently convinced the future is in manned space exploration and have already decided on baby Rey's career. They have already accepted the sacrifice baby Rey will make to bring our civilization to a better understanding of what is out there. Where we might go after we've fucked our planet arid and hopeless.

I had found all of space uninteresting until, in my last year of undergrad, I took a class with and became friends with and sometimes slept with a professor of astronomy who told me that my smoke was beautiful, that it was a gift to hold such power inside me. The fool didn't know what he was talking about, but he told me about the vastness of the universe, its knowns and unknowns—our singular beginning and the many, many ways our universe could end. I found peace in knowing this existence didn't have to be the only one. There was an alternate of myself who maybe spouted water instead of smoke. Every event of my life could have played out differently; every iteration of myself could be better than this one.

The gift giving. Amy offers up nothing. When it comes time for her turn, she says in her most serious tone, "My sparkling face is the only gift you need," which does not go over well with the other women, who scoff and make eye contact and twist the skin of their arms. Amy has taken to leaning against the wall and so I see her face fully for the first time. She looks like she's at the very end of recovering from a beating. Given how much she liked to fight in our teenage years, this shouldn't surprise me, but it does. My gaze is on her just-ballooned cheek when, after twelve years, she meets me eye to eye.

"Give me another sip, babe. I had a long drive."

June, satisfied with our offerings, begins the long task of standing. "Where from?" she asks.

"Paris."

Amy watches the room of women do the math, crinkle the skin between their eyebrows.

"In Texas."

All this time I haven't said a word to her, and now I can see her waiting, her eyes taking measurements all over me, ears ready to glean meaning from my words. All the ways I've stayed the same. That's why I'm grateful when June says it's time for a game.

"What do you think, ladies? "Guess Who" or "bobbing-for-pacifiers." Which should we do first?" June asks.

"Fuck," Amy is the first to say, "I forgot to bring a fucking photo."

"That's alright. You're not the only one. We'll do that one last."

"No, no, we can do the photo thing. Let me just grab one from Facebook," Amy says, pulling a phone out of her bra, and here I am vibrating, because of course I had looked Amy up on Facebook when I got her email, and the year before that, and before that, and before that, and nothing ever came up, which either meant she used a fake name or she had blocked me before we had ever connected on there.

For perhaps the hundredth time, my mind searches for some wrong thing I did, some cruel act that made Amy decide to treat me like this. I can't find one.

The smoke begins and I choke it down.

"Amy, honey, that isn't going to work unless we have a printer, which we don't. And anyway, everyone would be able to tell which is yours." June heads into the kitchen but hollers back. "Jordan forgot to bring one, too, so you two can just watch while we play."

I didn't bring a photo because I didn't have one. Parents are the ones to hang onto those, and with the both of them dead, my supply of early-life treasures ran dry years ago.

I realize Amy's careless mind presents an opening. If I can get her away from the rest of the group while everyone guesses whose primped baby face matches with whose primped thirty-something face, I might get Amy talking.

The bobbing game is long and boring. Everyone but me succeeds in grabbing a pacifier with their teeth on the first try. I bob and bob but the stupid things get away from me. The game ends, Amy skips her turn, and June disappears and reappears with a cork-board puzzle of infant photographs. I'm gearing myself up, suppressing the smoke, which comes with anxiety too, and figuring out my means of extraction when Amy's hand wraps around my wrist and pulls.

In the kitchen, Amy finds another bottle of champagne and doesn't ask June before holding the bottle at arm's length and letting the cork fly around the room. She refills my glass and doesn't take a drink before offering it to me.

"I'm actually alright," I say, because I have a two-hour drive back and I'm through with my driving-just-below-the-line days.

Amy drinks most of the glass and tops it off. She drowned herself in alcohol when we were teenagers, so I shouldn't be surprised as I watch her down the second glass and pour.

All the anticipation, the anger and stewing I've done, putters out as I watch her drink herself dizzy, and I begin heading back to the living room. My questions, I realize, don't matter anymore, because in Amy's mind there's been two seconds between when she left and now. She didn't miss me because I was never gone, and she won't be apologizing, because she merely stepped into the ether and came back too late. If I could hate her right now, I would.

"Wait," she tells me, as if today is thirteen years ago and every word she speaks is my guiding light. I make my slow return to her, smoke erupting out of my nose, through my gritted teeth, twirling up toward the smoke detector above June's refrigerator.

Anger isn't the trigger this time, I realize. I'm making an escape for myself, like a magician dropping below stage while the audience is distracted by the haze. Maybe I've had more control over this thing than I've thought. Come away, it tells me because I tell it. You've got the screen, now *go*.

"Okay, calm down," Amy says in too forfeiting a tone, waving her arms to dispel the air and prevent the detector going off. She tugs me through a hallway like she knows this house, out through a back door, the screen door banging, banging, and the cold hitting us in layers. She runs, practically pulling my arm out of its socket, to a shed she must have seen before because its white paint marks it as one with the weeping sky and ice-packed earth.

"You're still doing that, then," is all she can say when we're closed inside the ten-by-ten shed, shivering, catching our breaths. "Well, I didn't want to set off the alarms again. This is a good place to talk, yeah?"

"It's fucking cold."

"Then warm us up. You've got a fire in there somewhere. Use it."

The first alarm I ever set off—the summer between junior and senior year—that's what she means when she says she doesn't want to set off the alarms again.

One afternoon, tar-melting in its intensity, we snuck into the air-conditioned bliss of our school. We holed up in the high school teacher's lounge and emptied the refrigerator and exchanged our dreams of the future. College, careers, old-age sap stories. Amy said her dream was to get as far away from me as possible, a joke at the time, but still I fumed and set off the sprinklers and we ended up soppy and huddled in the dark of a nearby closet as the janitors tried figuring out what had caused the downpour. They never found us.

That was before we ever kissed, before we really knew what it meant to share body heat, to feel the tremors of post-orgasmic release. We stayed there in the dark, shivering, shoulders pressed, laughs no more than whispers, until dark.

Thinking of then stops the smoke, smothers my fire just when we need it most.

Amy cradles her back against the hard corner of June's husband's worktable. This shed, Amy says, is where June's husband likes to go when he's tired of his pregnant wife and her wanting.

I want to ask her how she knows this, but I don't.

"So?" she says, her face rippling against the cold.

"You brought *me* here."

I look around the shed for a space heater, because no man however glued to masculinity can spend his hours in a ball-shrinking freeze like this. Nestled by a tool cabinet, I find one of those fireplace-shaped heaters and switch it on.

"God, you're a genius," Amy says, and before I can ask why we're here, she's hugging me, pressing her whole front to mine, wrists circling the back of my neck, breath acrid and muted by the winter air. I don't hug her back and I don't think she expects me to.

"How have you been?" I ask when she backs off.

She laughs and produces a cigarette from her pocket. "Do you really want to know?"

I see for the first time a gold ring fitted around Amy's finger. "You're married," I say, more a question than a statement.

She flicks her cigarette ash onto June's husband's concrete floor.

"Divorced, or on my way there—" She wrestles the ring off and chucks it toward me like I'm someone who catches things. It lands on the ground between my feet, molar-sized diamond buried from view. I leave it there, even though I've done the math and that kind of glint could cover my rent for three years and then some. "—Asshole tried to demand it back. It's yours. I didn't want it, but I wasn't giving it back."

"So the fancy car, " I say. Was it his?"

Amy's fingering a C-clamp at her end of the worktable. "No." Like that's a proper response. I wonder if Amy has a lineup of rich boys or men or women keeping her afloat. "It was just an Uber."

"What kind of Uber driver can afford a Tesla?"

Amy winds the lever; the clamp slams down.

"Okay, fine. It is mine. My driver, my car. I'd usually drive myself, but I fucking hate this weather." She's combing over her hands now, the ghost of her wedding ring having barely paled against her skin. "I fight, okay? Not UFC or anything."

"Funny," I say, not laughing.

"I'm serious. Bantamweight, though they're trying to push me down to the flies. Husband begged me to quit; didn't like me messing up my pretty face."

"Fucker."

"That's right. And anyway, I've got some wealthy private clients who overpay me. Boxing, Pilates, yoga. You name it."

"In Paris?" We have both gravitated to the space heater, our toes planted right under the thing.

"In L.A. Husband took me down to Paris to show me the money to be made in ranching. Told him to fuck off, said it was over, and headed straight north to here. He said ranching would be just like the farm. Didn't know what he was talking about."

"That's right." We farm girls don't consort with those types. Ranchers.

Amy, on her third cigarette since we've stepped in here, stoops down and lets her face burn against the faux fire.

"And you. What have you done with yourself? I mean, things couldn't have been too bad. You look the exact same."

I don't acknowledge her compliments because they have never been rooted in truth.

"I work as an assistant editor for an academic journal."

"Well look at you. What's it called? I want to read it."

"The American Review of Physical Sciences."

"Fuck."

"I'm a glorified proofreader," I say and move my feet away from hers. "I wouldn't have gotten the job except for a professor recommending me."

In truth, the professor has been the one constant in my adult life. His texts come late at night or sometimes midday, weeks or sometimes months or years apart. Always, he asks for nudes (which I never give) and for astronomically themed sex talk (I'd love to travel through your wormhole, orbit your moons) and pretends he doesn't have a girlfriend, a fiancée, a wife. I pretend our short-lived, awkward intimacy is fulfilling.

In another universe, I have never spewed smoke or loved Amy or fucked a married man.

Amy's mouth curves and her lipstick wrinkles.

"Did you sleep with him?"

"I never said it was a man." Still, she tries to crush my toes with hers and I avoid her. "If you'd gone to college, maybe you wouldn't be so sexist."

"You're right. You know me. I hate other women. And men. And children. The only person I don't hate—."

"Why are we here?" I ask her, my patience imploding. The cold shoots through us now, and I don't know how she can continue to lie when we're halfway frozen. She coughs her smoker's cough instead of finishing her statement.

When she can breathe again, she replies, "Because you were about to set off the fucking alarm." She knows that isn't what I mean, and she gives herself a second before claiming, "I don't know. Why are you here, Jordan? You didn't have to come."

"You told me to," I say. I'm vibrating again, practically nebulous.

A cheer erupts from the house, muffled by the many walls between us and them.

"I did?" Amy asks, because she hasn't realized I won't accept her dishonesty any longer.

In a fraction of a second—I can't control it—the smoke races out of me. I haven't even opened my mouth and the whole shed is filled. Amy thinks to open the door, fan the smoke outdoors, but the cold and sleet convince her otherwise, so we're standing here, invisible to each other amid the smog.

I cough and choke and Amy does, too. Finally, I open the door. Rush out. Amy is slow to follow.

Already the flames, which for once licked up my throat, seared my tongue, are receding. Already, my breath clears. I've done this, I see now, to snap Amy out of herself. To wake her up from whatever dream she thought awaited her here. I feel guilt, knowing that for once my trick worked. She is changed.

"I'm sorry," she says, her voice not her own.

"What?"

We've caught our breath now and the shed is mostly emptied and the snow is stripping us to our atoms, so we step back inside, seal the door, and sit huddled around the heater.

"I fucked it up," she says, her eyes red and cheeks rosy now, too. "I wanted to see you, okay, but I also didn't. I was scared." She wipes her jaw, which trembles, and accidentally smudges her lipstick. "You don't forgive people. We both know that. I thought if I played it right you wouldn't get mad. I didn't think I could take seeing how much you hated me."

I tell her I don't hate her and I believe she believes me.

Something switched off in Amy as we cleared our lungs, and I begin to worry. I feel her heat, shedding itself from her now, and I know that she has outlived her star phase and become a red giant, massive and unstable. She's engulfing me now, cinder breath and salty rivers on my neck. She shivers, like all celestial bodies do, and says for a fourth of fifth time, I can't remember, how sorry she is. Her fingers press into my ribs like someone's gravity is pulling her elsewhere. She's missed me all this time and now she's come at the end, she says.

In most theories of how the universe will end, it is also reborn. The end brings the beginning, an infinite cycle of expansion and contraction. I tell her this but she isn't moved, and so I kiss her.

Her lips are burning coals against mine and her tongue a fast-melting meteor. Still, she shakes, she grows. She sucks the air from my lungs, a sudden, desperate attempt—pulls, pulls, pulls, until we can feel the little flames, the ashy bits of me fluttering between our mouths. We both hear it. A snap, a sizzle, somewhere deep inside me, and so she pulls back and smiles, believing she's done a good thing, and maybe she has. I love her for trying and hate her because it worked. I exhale and already I see the difference. A charcoal plume, brief, coils between us until my breath clarifies and my body becomes weightless. Stripped of mass, all energy. I kiss her again and feel her fusion, so powerful from this distance. I think maybe this isn't the end of things, but another BANG, another chance.

The front door to June's house heaves open and booms shut. A ripple shakes the inch-wide walls of our shed. We pause, consider that we've outstayed the party, or maybe June's husband has returned early. Silence follows and we look at ourselves, so altered from where we began, from where we were twenty minutes ago. We smile at each other, but we both know something is coming. We can feel it in the air and under our feet. Desperate for one another's warmth, we cling together.

I.

THROUGH the closed door, we hear a woman's cry. In the bedroom, we find June alone. The guests have left. She sits on the bed, its padded corner dipping under her stellar mass, condensing, pulling us in. Baby Rey is coming, she tells us. Breathe, we tell her. In, in; out, out. One breath is all it takes: the birth and death of the universe. *Inhale:* BANG—all scatters, convenes to form stars and planets and you and me. *Exhale:* SWOOSH— we've come so far that the only way forward is back. Back, back, back, until we're one gooey mess again. After, Amy takes care of the sheets. I clean and wrap the baby in the finest cloth. A door opens and Mr. Albright, June's husband, greets his newborn daughter with wet eyes and gentle hands. All the guests return, bring family and friends and all the bright faces of the world until we're shoulder to shoulder. A million worlds were birthed and died as baby Rey entered this world. A million Amys and a million Junes and a million Jordans and in all of them we are together, joined by this moment.

II.

THE door to the toolshed booms open. Wood against wood. Everything has drawn so far from everything else, atoms all across the universe split, welcoming renewal in a different face. Amy's hand up my shirt, Mr. Albright, June's husband, with this hands on the doorframe like he's bracing himself to jump. He's plainer than I expected. Mean face if you've ever seen one, but you already knew that. He's filling our little shed with white smoke, fluorescent against the cold. Who are you? What are you doing? Where is my wife? Where is my baby? You are the only ones left, don't you know? I come home to find my house empty and you here, treating my home like it's yours. He grabs a hammer, like that will do any of us any good. We are less than atoms, light years apart now. Where is my baby? Where is my wife? What are you doing? *Who are you?*

III.

THE door neither closes nor opens. Amy pulls her head back and with still dream-laced eyes sees Mr. Albright, June's husband, watching from the corner of the room. How long have you been here? An open smile. Crossed arms. Or maybe it's the professor who appears, hands placed on our shoulders. The universe ends in a big slurp; a surprise bubble from some other world, sucking us in. Mr. Albright, or maybe the professor, has a proposition. We laugh and laugh and laugh, already sucked in, already hand-in-hand-in-hand.

IV.

THE space heater putters off. The door jams. Just when we needed your little fire, I kill it, Amy says. We huddle close. Strip down, touch skin to skin anywhere we can, until there's no warmth left in us. The end of the universe: one lonely, lightless, sun-depraved existence. The universe dies for good. Stays dead for all eternity. We consider breaking the door down, throwing the dumb heater and June's husband's tools until we have an out, but we know, already, that we have drifted too far. We might die of exposure, she says, but at least our bones will be here, together, forever.

V.

AMY and I return to the party, which has grown in luster. June notices our clasped hands and shared lipstick and takes the both of us in one white-hot hug. The universe neither dies nor is reborn. Where we are now is where we will always be: an expansion seen through to its end. Mr. Albright, June's husband, walks in the front door to see his wife sharing a moment with friends, and for once he sees her radiance. Her beauty. He joins us in the hug, and baby Rey kicks, the force of her felt in all of us. This is love, I know and Amy knows and June knows. This is love. This is love. This is love.

Beginnings

The Brother

BEGINNINGS

I EXPECTED the sun. I didn't expect the space, the plush carpeting, the way the light paves golden rivers across the wall at dawn. I've never been an early riser. My mother and my sister and I— when we lived together, when Mom was still alive and Jordan wasn't backpacking cross-country with her newfound (re-found?), still-married girlfriend—had always stayed up 'til dawn. Not woken to it but greeted its face, fixing the horizon before we took to our beds. Now, I am alone. I wake in my ex's guest bedroom, because even in his absence, I can't breech that barrier, mend the broken and call it my own.

Rafael's plane, I imagine, burrows above the Atlantic as I watch sunlight flay his walls and warm his rooms. There are many. I haven't counted, but his house contains at least three bedrooms and a study, a living room, a sunroom, a kitchen, and two bathrooms. A basement. This luxury was inconceivable when we dated. Maybe it's that he didn't look for better jobs when we were together. Maybe it's that I was a bigger drain on his wallet—starving artist—than either of us realized. Either way, our sinking, moldy, one-bedroom apartment pales in comparison. In my first twelve hours of house-sitting—which will involve caring after Raf's two cats and dozens of plants—I haven't ventured past the guest bedroom, living room, and kitchen, because a demon lies in these shadows, ready to sink its fangs into my feet.

Still, I awake hopesheared.

Rafael owns two cats, the biter and the runner. These are new additions to his life, too. We were petless in our two years together, mostly because we couldn't afford them, or at least I thought we couldn't afford them. Already, the runner—Flea—has zipped through my ankles a dozen times, booted paws swishing against the shag, black body a blur. The biter, on the other hand, has yet to show his face. I know from Raf's Facebook posts that he is all gray fur and over-round blue-green eyes and thin lips marked by a snaggle-tooth. Even before Raf left for his flight, the biter didn't show.

In those five minutes Raf and I spent together last night, exchanging keys and cash for cat food and Google Sheets for his plants (no kidding), he barely made eye contact. His voice lilted softer than usual, and he hovered close, like how we had stood at parties, at events, in line. His finger would hook into my belt loop, pull me close, so that we stayed literally attached at the hip, always. In those few minutes last night, I felt warm air swell between us. How quickly body heat amplifies in close quarters. I felt, in his warmth, his non-look, his proximity, that he was signaling something, something important and concrete that should either buoy or sink me over these nine weeks, but we only shared five minutes together and instead of surety I floundered, as I always do. He left and I was struck with the same feelings his final words spurred during our break-up a year ago—confused, disappointed, hot. He left, and the biter stayed hidden, and the runner grazed my ankles over and over and only when I switched off the lights and crawled into bed did he calm. Now, I wake to a new, golden world all my own.

No more floundering. You are earthbound. Act like it.

And so I get up and wander into every room of this too-big house and name each corner mine. I look for the biter, demon or not, and instead find treasures: old VHS tapes and sun-bleached magazines and long-forgotten Halloween candy. I take them all as my own and gorge myself on sugar and nostalgia. I tell myself this gig will be good for me. Nine weeks of solitude to collect my ill-mended bones, and dry, lifeless skin, and blood-shot eyes and reform myself.

The last thing Raf told me after we broke up: "It weighs too much, being loved by you. You haven't even loved yourself—you can't put that on me too."

And it had hurt.

And it had taken months to forgive him.

And so, we had no contact between those words and his request just two weeks ago.

Now, he texts to remind me to check his Google Sheet for my itinerary, and I do. I find he has written whole biographies for each plant and each cat. Has written down watering and feeding schedules by the minute.

From his bio, I learn that Bear, the biter, had his snaggle tooth long before Raf adopted him as a stray—the vet had poked at its whittled point, sharpened but weakened, before Bear sunk its end deep into the vet's thumb. The runner, Flea, had been adopted soon after, and named for his black fur and unmatched speed.

And so I stop my search. I put on socks and indoor shoes, each anxious step like holding a hand to a monkey's cage. Still, he doesn't show.

And I brew Raf's coffee and eat Raf's eggs and consider what post-reform Chung may look like. How Raf might fit, or not, in New Chung's life. I debate. Do I spend these nine weeks looking for jobs and apartments for lease? Do I accept that Raf's kindness, this freedom he has granted me, is kindness only?

—But before I flesh out my desired result, give it a name, Bear, biter, stray, alien, leaps to the couch's top, inches from my face.

Brr-up.

I don't look at him. His big, fish-bowl eyes stare at me.

Never look a cat in the eyes, my sister always says. They take it as a threat. A challenge. On the farm—where my sister and I had grown up, before our parents split and our father died and our mother died and she and I became less and less our old, lake-sodden selves—our cats, the dozens of them, had never attacked us. As my sister would also say, they had been lulled to submission by the gods or whatever she pretended gave meaning to our dissolving, dissolving, dissolving lives, and so we were saved the cuts and bites and rabies shots in our young age.

Brr-up.

I don't turn my head, but I do follow my sister's advice.

Lower my head, close my eyes and open them slowly, affectionately, with my gaze leveled toward his chest. The cat's blink. His love you, Boo.

He yawns, and in my periphery, I see his nail-sharp fang catch the sunlight. I cringe.

He sprints away.

Before I've finished my coffee, Raf lights up my phone again.
Made it to London. 5-hr layaway. Shoot me.
I wait twenty minutes, and then I text back. *Only if you shoot me first.*

IN the sunroom, I assess my work. Ferns and lilies and succulents and herbs. I water, mist, shade, shift. I update the Google Sheet with my work and try to remember which name applies to which plant. He's never been able to resist the opportunity. When we were together, Raf named our cars, our bed, our coffee cups, and our boxes of wine. He thrived on melodrama. *How dare you rinse out Theo before I finished my coffee? Beauregard hates you, you know.* Our front-door mat. *He knows you step around him.* Even now, I can't just dash water over a cacti or basil or dill or spider plant. I know the significance of names, and that he named all living, dead, and inanimate things, while he only ever called me *You* doesn't miss me.

When I was at my worst, when I really did wish for Raf to just leave, to just fuck off, I would think of his Ma and Pa. How steeped in goodness, love and warm hugs they had been. How if such grounded, well-intending people had raised him, then surely his more rage-fueled, clawing bouts were only a step in his long trail to their light.

Jordan would set me right anytime I told her this.

"Fuck journeys, you don't have to be his stepping-stone."

But she believes every other person is a threat. As far as I know, she's made few exceptions. Even now she texts me—checks in on me.

No I haven't invited any randos in. No I haven't walked these streets alone. No. No. No. I'll be fine.

And she sends me TikTok stories of people randomly attacked on subways, on hiking trails, in their own apartment hallway, and I don't fight, I don't mention that that rarely happens here, in our little Midwestern college town.

Outside the glass walls, I watch a vole scurry toward the door. He scrabbles for an entrance, an escape from the cold. Today is New Year's, the beginning of a decade, and a part of me knows I should let the little beast in. A part of me knows this house sitting is just house sitting. These weeks are too short. My own parents couldn't change so how will I? How can I hope for a thing that requires so much movement on both sides.

I slide the glass door open, leave an opening three fingers wide, just enough to welcome the vole in, just enough to keep the cold out.

I spend the first morning of a new decade awash in light, knotted back to cool linoleum, lungs fresh with oxygen, tongue singed with bitter. The vole nests against a bag of fertilizer and when it's settled, we sleep.

HOURS later, I wake to chilled-white toes and sweat-swathed skin and find the vole gone and the door, the sunroom door leading to a graveled alley, still open. No. More open than I had left it. Maybe.

My skin feels heavy over my bones, all those UV rays amplified by the glass. I shuffle to the hefty metal sink near the entry to the house and bend my head under its faucet. I drink and drink and drink and think and think and think. Had the sunroom-to-house door been shut when I dozed off? Just because I didn't see the biter or the runner, I can't say they weren't in the room.

I scramble, shut the door, search the house, every room, every closet, the dust-swathed underside of every couch and bed. The runner sleeps in a cabinet. The biter. The biter is nowhere to be found.

I DEBATE a dozen times whether it's better to text Raf or let him begin his vacation undisturbed. Every room. Every inch. I've gone over them a dozen times before the sun scrapes through western windows. My palms go sore from bracing my body against shag carpeting, against tile, against the cold, cold gravel of the alley. The biter refuses to show himself.

As night nears, I hope that he, wherever the fucker went, will be frightened into returning. His home is warm and full with food and good water and good vibes.

"Please, dear god, come home."

As we near midnight, the runner and I, I decide on leaving the sunroom-to-alley door open, closing the sunroom-to-house door, and fixing strings across the entry, bells aloft, visitors announced by the soft tinning of metal against metal. I grab Raf's box fan, run it in the sunroom. Tape an open bag of treats to it. Pray.

I sit in the living room just ten feet away, play *The Return of the King* on silent just to fill the time, and wait, breathe, check the sunroom minute after minute. Nothing. I watch *The Hobbit* (the first and only watchable one). Feed in the second *Hobbit,* because, whatever. He doesn't show. Put on the third and feel the sun's heat blister across my face, flare up my dried and livid skin. I keep my eyes open. Halfway into Smaug's descent, the couch beside me shifts.

Brr-up.

The biter. Bear. I freeze. We've locked eyes. No thoughts existed between his chirp and this exchange, and I sweat. I swallow, cotton-mouthed.

Brr-up.

He rushes to my side and, like water, rubs against my arm, furious, softer than I could've dreamed. He lays over my hand. He looks at me.

Brr-up.

I pet his head and watch Smaug gore a village, cast children to ash.

FOR the last eight months I have lived off others' generosity. First came the six-month artist residency a small Midwestern art center had granted me, padded with free meals and lodgings and a fully stocked print studio. After that ended in November, Jordan let me finish out her lease, rent pre-paid, as she traipsed through the West with Amy. I'd sold enough work during the residency, all cheap, unimaginative prints of prairie skies and broken limbs and damp, damp earth, and that has fed me, kept the lights on. It also helps that Raf left a packed fridge, freezer, and pantry, too.

Occasionally, I visit the final product of my residency, its airy, paper-thin figure suspended in the basement. All those months wasted, until I made one good work. One I can't even think to sell. One that galleries aren't likely to show.

It mirrors me, the figure, a trick of air and strings and light, but you already knew that.

I name it, because all things in this house must be named. I leave it in the dark, cool shadows of the basement because its frail skin yellows so easily. I keep the door closed because the cats are a sure predator. I lock the door so that I am less likely to visit it too often. Saturate its silhouette in my mind and render it ordinary.

AUSTRALIA burns. A map floods with cartoonish flames across that hell-borne continent. Fire-licked streets, burned koalas curl away from screens, snakes run for the cities, infest houses and storefronts and gas stations.

And Raf's texts keep coming:

Who knew Venice could bore you to tears.

My Ma won't stop croaking about what loneliness does to the body. About cold beds. About you.

What are you up to?

How's Flea? How's Bear?

Send me pictures, and don't you dare leave yourself out.

And usually I respond. I let time stretch between us, enough to make him wonder. The conversations stay harmless, stay vague, stay unresolved.

Bear and Flea prove to be my perfect housemates. The biter, Bear, became my bedside companion, my couch buddy, after those first two days, as if all those hours had been a test, and I had passed. In his unexpected calm, he would lie on his side on the shag, stretch his front legs in a long, furry arc toward me. He lies on his back often, his fluffy stomach inviting, his snaggle tooth a faint reminder.

For days, weeks, I don't leave the house except for groceries, the mail, plant fertilizer when necessary. I wrap myself tight in my own isolation. Keep my phone close. Order delivery, all the rich, glistening foods I missed while I was eating the free shitty cafeteria food during my residency and the rich-but-disgusting canned and boxed foods Jordan had left me at her place. All that time, I saved my money, the few hundreds of it, and pretended that this liberty, this good fortune, could continue on indefinitely.

As part of my rest and relaxation, I keep off Facebook and Twitter and Instagram. Not that I ever used them much before. I journal, which I've never done, because my mother would have certainly read them and my sister would have definitely read them and I've generally always worried that writing down anything unformed in my head makes them solid, rocky, and no amount of chiseling can change the course.

I write about the cats. About the figure in the basement. About my mother and father and grandparents and uncle, dredging up the dead. I write about my sister and I write about Raf and his parents, who are too good for him and for me and for the world.

I watch movies, all the ones my mother and I marathoned years ago—the kung fu flicks and the gritty action adventures and the cheesy romantic comedies with that early aughts low-rise, glossy-lipped sheen. I order Thai and Korean and Italian and once or twice walk the half-mile to downtown and eat my ramen solo, facing the window, the street, reminding myself of the richness I am abstaining from. The faces I wrote off only to satisfy Raf, to satisfy my sister—every stumbling college kid and wide-eyed teen and eyes-to-asphalt townie that has worked every restaurant and bar and coffee shop job in town, their faces mingling in the back of everyone's mind as the years grow and their back aches and feet flatten. I watch and enjoy my Tonkatsu Hokkaido and sake and keep to myself.

Flea and Bear and Marcus, which is the name I've given the vole after all these weeks, lick my takeout containers clean. Each day creeps like molasses, a sweet, weighty treat. I begin to hope against reality. Forge unlikely futures. I send Raf photos of our little friends (Marcus out of view, because Raf's musophobia used to send him into the fetal position for ungodly amounts of time), and he sends me photos of Milan, of Il Duomo and all the city's incredibly beautiful, incredibly old and massive structures.

The day that Kobe Bryant, his daughter, and seven others die in a fiery crash, I wake to a red sky and the sunroom drain backed up. According to Raf's calendar, today is cleaning day and I think myself lucky, this sludge perfectly timed. After I've sopped up its spittle, I transfer each clay pot, the twenty of them, to the alley and sweep, mop, and bleach the floor. I identify the plants ready for repotting. I assess the damage of the mold which, for a time, had begun its invisible work of tainting one corner of the room. Transfer all the pots back to their spots in the sunroom. After weeks away, I hop on Instagram. Think to post a photo of all this good work until, like all good things, this beauty spoils. Raf's posts populate my screen. Top of them all: A mouth-on-mouth kiss with a translucent, pink-eyed blond I've never seen before. The photo is grotesque, tongues and meaty insides-of-the-mouth in frame. The sun peeks between their noses and alights the man's long, curling nose hairs.

I drop the phone. Curse myself.

I kick the phone. Crack its screen with velocity.

For the rest of the day, I languish on the couch, movie after shitty movie, and let Bear curl against my stomach, purr away my heart.

Raf texts, comments in his spreadsheet.

It's cleaning day Boo. Don't forget! When I don't respond: *Hey, hope everything's okay.* And *Send me pics! Need your dumb little faces today.*

Days pass and I spend as little time at the house as possible. I journal at coffee shops, thumb through new books at the library, drink myself sideways and wake to red-eyed bartenders giving me the *please-don't-make-this-a-thing-please-i'm-sorry-you-need-to-go-i-just-work-here-to-pay-off-my-debt-from-that-one-time-i-maybe-sort-of-swallowed-a-lot-of-sleeping-pills-and-wished-the-abyss-away-i-just-work-here-to-feed-my-cat-i-just-work-here-so-can-you-please-go-and-don't-hate-me-i-hate-me-and-you-hate-you-so-we're-two-fish-stuck-in-the-same-boat-really-please-just-go-in-peace-go-in-peace-go-in-peace* look.

And I feed Flea and Bear and Marcus, I do. I clean their litter boxes and sweep up Marcus's coarse-ground poops. But the sunroom. I seal it off. I cannot go in.

FIVE-AND-A-HALF weeks into my stay, I return to the streets, showered and clean-shaven and ready to push past the gloom, kick up dirt in my wake. I've reverted to my nocturnal self, and so I don't make it out until sunset. Grab dinner for breakfast at the brewery, fill up on oaty stouts and, when I leave, stumble into lines of people entering the local movie theater a few stores down.

"What's going on?"

"What do you think?" A woman wearing a frizzy blond-curls wig and a low-cut, high-slit red gown says, striking a pose. "Sorry, is that rude?" She touches her hand to my back and presses, ushering me inside. "It's the Oscars watch party! Have you ever been before?" When I shake my head, she continues, "You're gonna have fun, Hun. You *can* sit with us," she says, a riff on one of the dozens of early aughts movies I've rewatched while at Raf's. "Here," and she hands me a sheet of paper, award categories and nominees printed in as unmannered an order as possible. She tells me it's our chance at a $100 gift card and free concessions for a year.

"I haven't seen any of these."

"Don't worry," a guy rocking a *Pulp Fiction* Travolta look says as he dances over. "DiCaprio is a sure for Best Actor and, let's see. Best Director, Tarantino."

The woman in the red dress laughs. "Biased. No, no, no," she says, assessing our work. "Bong Joon Ho for Director and *Parasite* for Best Picture."

"No, no, no," the man says, wagging his finger. "She's just trying to get you on her good side." When I shake my head, he choke-laughs, face bubbling red. "I just meant because you're—"

"Don't listen to him," the woman says.

We submit our guesses and as we head upstairs for the plushy balcony seats, the man wraps an arm around my and the woman's necks. My skin curdles. I realize I haven't been touched by another person in at least eight months, maybe longer—those last few months where Raf and I were together distant. Us, two ghosts haunting one another. Several others wait for us upstairs. Another woman wears washed-out old-timey men's clothes—a vest, suspenders, pants.

"Jo!" the blond chimes, sliding into her lap. Smearing her lipstick with a kiss.

"Be worthy love," Jo says.

"And love will come," the blond replies.

"Who's this?"

"Oh, uh," the blond says, squinting her eyes at me. "What's your—,"

"Look at his hair!" another man in a soldier's uniform replies, "Same cut. You can be Ki-Woo."

"Heh." I sit between him and Travolta and take their free wine.

They let me in on the nominees, the treasures I've missed and bait films I can skip. Slowly, each winner steps on stage, tries to beat the music. Slowly, *Parasite,* Korean-language thriller, wins award after award, Bong Joon Ho returning to the stage one, two, three times. As Best Picture nominee teasers play on screen, everyone tenses. Each *Parasite* win has elicited theater-wide cheers and applause. High-pitched screams.

The hosts hesitate. The world stops.

And *Parasite* wins. Best Picture, Director, Screenplay, International Film.

The theater goes crazy. The soldier and Travolta and the blond and Jo rave. Shake me. "Ki-Woo! Ki-Woo! You did it, you son of a bitch!"

And I take their high fives and hugs. Eat their popcorn.

And the high of our win is so strong and the night so young and our throats so parched that I say fuck it. I invite them over to the house and we arrive, each of us tripping and stumbling along the way.

I rummage around the pantry until I find the champagne bottles Raf has stashed there. He doesn't own flutes, so we fill coffee mugs and shot glasses.

"Damn, are you rich?" Travolta asks me.

"Oh yeah." I stumble into the couch, spilling my drink over its back.

Someone puts on bad music and that's the thing, I think, about this moment. The cheap costumes and the bad booze and the music. The Ki-Woos. Heh. And the You're a Winner! Heh. And the queer feeling of these strangers' hot breath swirling around my head.

We party for hours, past midnight. At some point, someone puts on Parasite, and though I know I should give it its due, sit and watch and absorb, I don't. I dance. I take sloppy selfies with each of them and contemplate having them tag me. Let that populate Raf's feed. But I don't.

As we're hitting our second wave, as I look to the TV and see a man's oily forehead and wild eyes poke up from the basement stairs, the blond rushes in. "Look at these cuties!" she yells, chasing the runner into our foot space.

"Whoa!" the soldier yells.

"Fast fucker!" Travolta laughs, reaching for him, too late. He falls face-first into the carpet.

"Wait, is it chasing something?"

Time slows, or my eyes accelerate—the vole's clumsy scramble, the runner's determined sprint, the look of horror dawning on every other person's face but my own.

Mouse! Mouse!

The soldier is the first one to the door. "Ew, ew, ew," the blond whines. The others follow. No goodbyes. No thanks. No sorry for leaving. Fuckers. They flee, leave the door gaping open. My brain lags, hands tingle, stomach turns.

I find the biter in his hiding spot, the vole in the kitchen catching his breath.

I search for the runner. The runner is nowhere to be found.

THREE days pass, every telephone pole flyered and door knocked on. I stay off the lost pet Facebook groups, because I can't guarantee Raf won't see my post.

My phone screen is a puzzle of colors and lines, and so I put my email address on the *LOST CAT* flyers and stay an arm's length from my laptop at all times.

A week passes. Two. I turn to lying on the earth and peering into crawl spaces, under vehicles, mining old storage sheds, cavernous storm drains. I attempt damage control on Raf's plants, too, the more withered of which are slowly regaining their color.

I haven't checked Raf's spreadsheet since the day I saw his Insta, and though I've heard my phone's chime a few dozen times, I have no way of seeing what horror awaits me there. Finally, a week before Raf is supposed to return, I post in all the Facebook Lost Pet groups, on Craigslist, anywhere I can. Nothing. Big hearts and shares and encouraging words, but nothing meaningful comes.

And then I get a video call request through my email. It's Raf. The subject reads *STUCK OUTSIDE US: Can you stay?*

I accept the invite. Open the call.

In a grainy, low-lit rectangle, Raf's face comes to me hollowed out, eyes doubled from crying.

"It's my Ma," he says. He shakes, crushes his face. "She's on a ventilator, not sure how long she can stay on."

When I ask him what's happened to her, he looks into his camera, jaw dropped. Haven't I watched the news? I tell him I've been pre-occupied. There's a virus flooding hospitals in northern Italy, his whole family has gotten it. His grandpa already passed. His sister's working crazy hours at the clinic. He says they've run out of morgue space, they've run out of ventilators, they've run out of staff.

"I'm sorry," is all I can say. I can't look at him. He's no Raf I've ever seen before.

"I've been texting you. Tried to tell you last week."

"I dropped my phone. I'm sorry."

He heaves. Through the screen, I feel his heat. The ragged rasp of his lungs as he breathes.

"Can you stay a few more weeks? Please? I don't even care about the plants anymore. Just look after my cats. Please. I don't have anyone else. Please."

"Of course," I tell him. He ends the call as his father's shadow enters the frame. In the same moment, the biter jumps into my lap. Chirps. He has grown distant, lethargic since the runner's disappearance.

Brr-up.

I pet his cheek, his forehead, his chin.

He makes eye contact with me.

Before I can stop him—I wouldn't stop him—he opens his jaw, pulls my thumb. Sinks his fang in deep.

IN the second week of March, the country locks down. Raf emails me again. His Ma made it out, if a little slower than usual. In the time since our call, I've broken away from the Lost Pet pages enough to catch up. The virus came out of China, they say. The Chinese released it from a lab, they say. Or ate bats and sent the whole world skidding, they say. The president calls it the China Virus and the world jeers.

Other than grocery shopping, I only leave the house to search, plead, pray that the runner turns up alive. I knock on doors, but people no longer answer. I ask other walkers on the sidewalk, but everyone crosses to the other side. I get it. I don't hate them for it. At the house, I keep the TV running, watch the same shitty re-runs of the same shitty shows in-between commercials. I starve myself, not by choice, but because nothing sits right. Like anything I take into my body spills over the top. Like I'm full of bullshit, stupid bullshit, and I am.

And I turn dark and twisted and grainy. I can't look at myself in the mirror any more for fear of scaring off whatever little part of me remains. I think of the figure in the basement. I think of glass and warm bath water and the dark. I can hear it, I think, the slow drainage sucking me down from the inside. It's always been there, but now it has a sound. It has an urgency. I run the TV constantly, the ceiling fans, play music from Raf's oversized speakers. Anything to drown out the noise.

And I dismantle the figure in the basement. Take its skin and bones to the alley and torch it.

I ignore my sister's calls. I spend every day in the sunroom, tending to the last untainted life I have hold of. The biter keeps his distance. The vole doesn't return.

Finally, one day, someone comments on my posts about the runner. Includes a photo of what very likely could be him. Says he was spotted just four blocks away, so I grab a flashlight. It's just past sunset. I bring a bag of treats, one of the runner's favorite toys, and the harness and leash Raf said he likes to wear, though I struggle to believe it.

I find the house he was spotted at. I try to seem as uncreepy as I can searching around another person's home.

I call his name, shake the treat bag. I beg. I cry, hands to gravel, skin pressed white.

A blur of black flashes in front of me. I stand. Drop everything.

The runner stops for a second. Looks at me from the end of the block. Before his muscles twitch, I sprint. He darts around the corner and I follow. Too slow. He's out of sight by the time I round the bend.

I speed-walk, try my best to find him before some distracted driver can rip through the street and hit him. Or me.

One, two, three blocks. I'm out of breath. Vision doubling, when I see someone coming from up the sidewalk. I heave and raise up my arms.

"Hey," I call. "Have you seen a black cat?"

I'm catching my breath and fighting dizziness when I see the figure approaching fast. I look at him, register an unfriendly face. A furrowed brow. Fists clenched.

I pause. See his quickening steps. I don't think, I don't have my bearings, but I turn and run. I run and run and eventually look back, our distance narrowing. I stumble on upturned concrete. Trip and fall hard, nose to asphalt, blood hot.

Like all the times before, I feel the lift, the shift that comes before the black. The man reaches me and though I should've passed out by now, his kicks ram deep into my stomach, rail my ribs, rattle my head. All this and I'm still here. Try to shield my face. Try to shove him away.

Try to— Try to— Try to—

PLEASE. *Please. Please. Give me the black.*

The brother woke tired. Starved. The air he breathed swelled thick with dust, thick with cold and waning light. Like the edge of the universe. Like the inhale before all universes are born.

The brother heard a voice low—like a trill, a hiss, a moan—and searched for its source, though he found none. Before him listed planets, swelled suns. Dust and gas and debris sped by him.

He listened.

The voice boomed, a chorus of all noises at once. Instead of words, it showed him the power resting here. How, like all living and dead things, he came from star stuff and would return to star stuff, and then it spooled out all richness and warmth and it took him back. Back to the seconds before his blip. Before his fall. His run. Before he lied to Raf. Before he lost the runner or watched the Oscars or met the vole or finished his residency. Before his mother died or his father died or they left the farm. Before he swam out into Wilson Lake that night twenty years before. Before his life and his sister's life and his parents' and grandparents' and humans and their little planet and their roaring sun and their spiraling corner of the universe. It brought him all the way back where there was any back to go to, and it let him sit there. Drift in any moment as long as he liked and he took his time. Hours passed or maybe days. Doors like polar ice opened all around him. His birth, the lake, his parents' deaths, his stay at Raf's. The seconds before his fall. All promise and finality. Take it all back. Or. Take you back. Or. Take the stay back. Or. Take the run back. Or. Take the fall back. Or. Keep it all and pass through that gate, star stuff and all his living done.

He stepped forward.

THE brother stumbled on upturned concrete. Skidded to a stop. Turned.

In the minutes and hours and weeks that would follow, he would find the runner, matted and thirsty, in a rusted toolshed and take him home. He would call and tell Raf the truth. He was sorry, for his failings, for not listening to him, for trying to love without living. He would call his sister. Tell her how much he loved her. How much work they had to do. They had so much living left to do. And millions would die and the world would burn, but still there was life and light and goodness. The brother and sister survived and kept on surviving, time a finger poking their wounds, and they learned to bear the pain and clutch tight to the living they had left. Shed their seconds skins. Lay in the glory of the sun, grass blanketing them.

But for now, the brother turned and faced the man chasing him. The sudden shock of his stopping startled the man into stillness. The brother saw his eyes, the pale hunger in them, and released his breath. For now, they were two men on a speck of time. Open hands and settling hearts.

Acknowledgments

MANY thanks to Whitney Terrell, Christie Hodgen, Michael Pritchett, Mitch Brian, Adam Desnoyers, Mary Klayder, Terry Anderson, Gary McClure, and Bill Gies, who encouraged me in every stage of my writing and made me a better writer. Thank you to MFA family at the University of Missouri-Kansas City. Many thanks to Michael, Aunt Rosie, and Aunt Jeanne for your support and love. Thank you to the Lawrence Art Center, Raven Bookstore, and the community writers who honored "Wilson Lake" all those years ago, providing the reassurance I needed to finish this book. Thank you to PJ Carlisle and all those at TRP. Special thanks to Vi Khi Nao, who selected *Churn* as the 2022 TRP George Garrett Fiction Prize Winner. Lastly, many thanks to the editors and literary journals that first published these stories. Thank you, Kimberly Willardson of *The Vincent Brothers Review,* Anna Cabe, Janelle Bassett, and Maureen Langloss of *Split Lip Magazine,* Barrett Warner of *Free State Review,* Tommy Dean & Kathy Fish of *Fractured Lit,* Marc Berley of *LitMag,* John Wang of *Potomac Review,* Chris Lowe of *McNeese Review, Yemassee Journal,* and Robert James Russell and Jeff Pfaller of *Midwestern Gothic.*

First Publication Credits

"Wilson Lake" first appeared in a slightly altered form as "Wilson Lake, 1999," in *Midwestern Gothic,* Issue 20.

"Godless" first appeared in a slightly altered form in *Potomac Review,* Issue 68.

"Communion at a Taco Bell in Gypsum, Kansas" first appeared in slightly altered form as "Taco Bell is Coming for Gypsum, Kansas" in *LitMag.*

"Kindling," first appeared in a slightly altered form as "No Gods, Only Suffering" in *McNeese Review,* vol. 58.

"Six Days of Peace," first appeared in *Split Lip Magazine Online,* Jan. 2023.

"Burn," first appeared in *Free State Review Online.*

"Clinton Lake" first appeared in a slightly altered form in *Yemassee,* 2020 October Monthly Spotlight.

"Grandma Kim at Forty-Five: a serigraph in four layers" appeared in *Fractured Lit* online and in *Fractured Lit Anthology I.*

"Rend, Sew," first appeared in *Vincent Brothers Review,* Issue 25.